Jack McCuddles

and

The Case

of the

Vampire Hamsters.

Scott A. Coleman

For Salem, the best cat that ever was.

CONTENTS

Chapter 1

I was born to do evil with my magical ability. I'm also the cutest cat in the world, in case you didn't know. I'm sure you imagine my life is perfect, but it isn't perfect. I ended up with a good witch called Susie and I never get the chance to do evil. Doing good spells doesn't pay very well and evil spells can make a witch very rich. Therefore, we are always poor.

Susie looks nothing like a witch with her ginger hair and freckles. You'd think a witch that doesn't look like a witch would be embarrassing enough, but that's not the bad part.

The Witching Council took her Witch License away from her. Susie was very upset, as she now needs lots of money that we don't have, to buy her license back.

She claims they took the license away because of me. You see a witch has no actual magical powers; it's a cat like me that has all the magic ability.

I can do all sorts of spells. I am the smartest and cutest magical cat in the world. But without permission from my witch Susie, I'm not allowed to do any spells. That's the law. But I had no choice. I had to break the law to save the world - twice I might add - and I paid the ultimate price for it, not her.

I lost all my fur. It was dreadful. I wasn't able to leave the apartment for a month and I was so cold and itchy waiting for my fur to grow back. I expected some sympathy from Susie, but oh no, all I got was her moaning about having to get a job to feed me and keep me warm.

I bet if I were your cat, you wouldn't moan about taking care of me. You'd just pet the white bit of fur under my chin, feed and cuddle me and buy me a nice soft velvet blanket to sleep in.

I deserve a better home to live in, and an owner that appreciates me. Not one that wakes me up at six in the morning to tell me "she" is going to work.

At that time of the morning, I am dreaming about winning the Cat of the Year competition. So, I don't really care where Susie is going, not that I actually know. She did tell me, but I was eating at the time.

I think she likes her new job. She is always singing at six in the morning about the Monday Blues or whatever day of the week it is Blues. I don't listen to the words of the song that she's singing. Instead, I make my own breakfast because as she says, every morning, "I am far too busy to make you breakfast and I have to go to That Hateful Place."

I don't know what she does there, but it is a funny name for a workplace.

Anyway, she has a job and sings a lot so at least she is happy. But, not me. I feel neglected by her and I must also make my own lunch and afternoon tea.

I hate waking up from my naps and having to make my own food. I did ask her to prepare my meals before she goes to work and all I got was a cold stare from her. Maybe she is getting a cold.

But that's not even the worst part of my life. That honor goes by the name of Charlie McMoose.

Charlie used to work for the Mice Police. They are an annoying bunch of mice that make sure magical cats don't perform magic illegally. He claims he lost his job helping me save the world (twice). He was there. But, I don't recall his help.

I don't like him. He's just a walking piece of stewing meat waiting for a pot.

He has his own bedroom in the apartment. I sleep in a broken basket on a cold and fake wooden floor in the kitchen and what's more, he has his own bed.

A bed! He is not even six inches high.

A shoebox is a mansion to the likes of him. Give him a bowl of water and he has his own swimming pool.

Now he calls himself a "sleuth."

I had to look that word up in the dictionary. It is a fancy word for a detective. Him a detective, that makes me laugh. He couldn't find a dust bunny if it was stuck to his nose. But wait it gets worse.

I am not allowed to stay in the apartment on my own, so, wait for it; I have to go to work with him.

Can you believe that?

I have to work for a living and with the so-called great sleuth Charlie McMoose. Me, the cutest cat in the world that should be loved, adored and pampered until I purr myself to sleep, has to help him solve mysteries.

I hate my life. I don't get my morning, afternoon or pre-dinner naps anymore. It is no wonder I am cranky all the time.

Take today for example. I had to make own breakfast.

There I was eating my pancakes with fake maple syrup, as we can't afford the real stuff, when McMoose runs into the kitchen shouting:

"McCuddles, we have a crime to solve."

"Great," I said, with my best fake smile.

I am so cute when I smile, even when it is fake, did I tell you that already?

"Yes McCuddles, a mystery to solve," he shouted, climbing up the table.

I feigned interest. "You said that already."

"Did I? I am so excited...a mystery McCuddles...a mystery."

He was wearing his best blue suit, although I think it is his only suit. He stuck his paws into the pocket of his blue waistcoat and removed his pocket watch. Why he can't wear one on his wrist is the only mystery I can be bothered to solve.

"We must leave presently," he said, glancing at the time on his watch.

I showed him all the enthusiasm I could muster. "Must we? When is presently?"

"The bus leaves-"

"Bus?"

"Yes, the bus leaves in ten minutes and then we catch the 11:09 train to Backwheretonowhere."

"I am not taking a bus, they are filthy, my fur, my beautiful fur will be ruined. And as for a train, I am not traveling in the baggage area."

"Tickets, Mcfuddles. I have tickets."

"My name is Jack McCuddles."

8

"I know that McMuddles, now come, we must leave presently."

"You said tickets. First Class?"

He removed a small slip of paper from his trouser pocket, "Fifth."

"There is no fifth," I screamed. "Even chickens get to travel third class."

"Come on McPuddles, we need to leave now."

"I take it that it's presently now."

"Yes," he said, slipping on his black bowler hat. "We have a mystery to solve."

"Yeah, so you keep saying, so who hired us?"

"Me," he said. "You work for me, and I was hired by Lord and Lady McBedbugs. They have some mysterious goings on in their hotel, The Flea Palace of Delight."

"Let me guess, the hotel is on the edge of a cliff and there's a cave that pirates used to hide their treasure in beneath the hotel and suddenly they have no customers and they are broke, penniless, cent-less and senseless. They must be if they hired you."

"You read about it in the newspapers?" he asked, lifting his umbrella off the table.

As if I would read anything that doesn't mention me. "No, I just guessed."

Actually, his umbrella is toothpick with some tarp glued to the top of it. Totally useless when it rains. I think he carries it for show. All he is missing is a briefcase, but he doesn't change his underwear often enough to carry one.

"Well for that matter," he said, looking rather smugly, "what...wasn't in the newspapers was...the mysterious bite...marks."

I hate when he pauses mid-sentence, it is a bit overly dramatic and hard to follow.

"Bite marks?" I asked him.

"Bites...Yes...Bites...Mcfuddles...Bites...Vam...pire...bites."

Van tire bites. I think he is a bit batty. I have never heard of such a thing.

"Can you believe it McCuddles, this will be my biggest mystery ever to solve," he said.

"Actually isn't this your first ever case as a sleu...detective?"

"That's not the point, they must have heard of my brilliance and that's why they called me and requested my expertise."

"Are we getting paid for this?"

"Of course, I am getting paid, how else can I help Susie pay the bills?"

"Well if you found a new home she would have one less mouth to feed."

"I eat less than you do."

"What about my nap?"

"What nap?"

"My after breakfast nap?"

"The trip is all expenses paid."

"What does that mean?"

"Free food, McStuffels."

I hate when he says my name wrong. "Free dinner?"

"Yes," he said smiling, "and what's more we get a free room in the hotel, with access to a sauna, gym, and a free all-you-can-eat breakfast."

The things I must do to get food. Most cats sit around all day napping and then look sad when they want food. But not me. I have to follow a stinking mouse around and act as his assistant for a meal.

At least, I will have free food, handed to me. I wonder how big the bed in the hotel will be. I suppose investigating van tires bites might not be such a bad a way to pass a few hours. All I had to do was survive using public transport and his company.

"When do we leave?" I asked him.

"Presently," he answered.

"That's now...right?"

"Yes McIdiot, now, right now, as in we have vampires to hunt."

"What? You never mentioned vampires."

"I did."

"You said van tires bites."

"Clean out your ears McFuddles."

I cleaned out my ears once his back was turned. Then I flicked the wax from my paw in his direction. Sadly, I missed him.

He jumped off the table and walked to the door. He climbed up the doorframe and jumped onto the door handle.

"Come on McFuddles, the mystery won't solve itself," he beamed.

Nor will he solve it. He doesn't even know where the bus stop is. I do, now that Susie and I are forbidden to use my magic. We have to use the bus instead of our broomstick.

I walked slowly to the door and looked at the proud mouse all set to solve his first mystery. He flipped his umbrella onto his shoulder and marched down the stairs and out of our apartment building.

I looked back at my basket. I had a horrible feeling I wasn't going to see it for some time.

I closed the door behind me and then I shivered. Vampires, blood-sucking vampires.

What kind of idiot goes looking for vampires?

I got my answer when I made it outside the apartment building.

"The bus," McMoose shouted. "Hurry or we will miss it."

Chapter 2

McMoose took the seat next to the window on the bus. I hate him. He can't even see out the window, he doesn't reach that high. He's so selfish. If I had the window seat, I could have looked at my reflection in the glass.

A cat as cute as me should never be denied the opportunity to stare at the wonder that is me. But then again it might have been dangerous, as my cuteness will distract the drivers of the cars passing by us.

The journey to the train station was one of the worst experiences of my life. The bus kept slowing down, stopping and then speeding up. I felt seasick and when it wasn't stopping it was crawling over the speed bumps. How I endured those ten minutes is beyond me.

I was so relieved when the bus pulled up across from the Endoftheline train station. McMoose gave our tickets to the large ticket inspector standing by the gates to the train platform.

"Are my suitcases loaded?" McMoose asked him, pointing at the waiting train.

"Yes sir," the ticket inspector replied, "the taxi arrived last night and your suitcases are in the baggage compartment."

"Thank you," McMoose said, tipping his hat at the ticket inspector. "Come on McCuddles the train won't wait all day for you."

I looked at McMoose. I wanted to snarl and rip his beady eyeballs out of his selfish head. He made me travel by bus when he had his suitcases delivered by taxi.

I followed slowly behind the pompous walking sandwich towards the train. Sadly, the train was already on the platform, halting the evil thoughts in my mind. I won't say any more, it wasn't a very nice thought that involved a moving train and a tripping mouse.

The train had six carriages and bellowing steam was coming

from the engine at the front. A tired looking man was shoveling coal into the bit on the engine where the coal goes.

"The train is steamed up," he shouted, "all aboard all that's traveling to destinations far away."

Far away? Maybe all the smoke and steam was getting to the poor chap, but after finding out McMoose had hired a taxi for his bags, I was a bit worried.

"What does he mean, far away?" I asked McMoose. "How far is far away?"

"Your carriage is down there, not far," he said, pointing to the last carriage.

"My carriage?"

"Did I not mention, I have a sleeper-car booked in First Class for myself, it will take a day to get to Backwheretonowhere. But don't worry McWuddles, I told the conductor to leave you a bowl of water and a blanket in your carriage."

My nails grew through my paws. I wanted to rip his stupid bowler hat and head off his even stupider shoulders. But before I was able to reach him, the whistle on the train screamed and so did the coal shoveling man.

"Get on now," he screamed, "if we don't leave the train will explode from the steam build-up."

I felt a hand grab my ears and fling me down the platform towards my carriage. I saw the look of joy on the ticket inspector's face before another hand came out of the open carriage door and pulled me inside.

The same hand flung me hurriedly down a dark and damp carriage. I fell onto a woolen blanket.

I hate woolen blankets. They itch and this one smelled used, the damp dog kind of used. Just as my eyes adjusted to the dark of the carriage, a single light bulb extending from a cord in the ceiling came on.

The light bulb swung like a pendulum as the train pulled away from the station. I heard the latch close, on the door of my carriage. I knew this was to be my prison until we arrived at the Backwheretonowhere train station.

I surveyed my prison. The smell of damp dog was everywhere. A small bowl of water and some crusty bread lay beside the itchy woolen blanket. I looked into the bowl and saw that a few flies had lost their lives to the water.

The bread was all blue moldy. A small team of maggots was departing from the bread in search of a tastier meal. They slithered across the floor past me in the directions of some cracks in the wooden floor.

The floor wasn't much better to eat from, judging by the upturned wood lice in the corner of the carriage. I wanted to cry. I look cute when I cry, but I look cute all the time, so crying wasn't the solution to my problem. I had to find a way out of this carriage and find some food.

I was starving. I hadn't eaten in over an hour.

I walked carefully to the door of the carriage, seeking a new home and trying to avoid the few surviving insects. I jumped onto the rusty door handle. It didn't budge. The door was locked. I had neither key nor the strength to break the door down.

Now I know I needed Susie's permission to perform a magical spell to open the door. However, Susie isn't technically a witch anymore. So I figured, as I have nobody to ask permission from, that I could use my magic powers. And if nobody heard me then who would know?

I looked over my shoulder, just in case. I didn't expect to see anyone, but you can never be too sure. I looked back at the door and I waved my right paw in the air.

"Meow meow open the door meow meow," I whispered, waving my right paw at the door handle.

The spell worked. The carriage door slowly opened.

Food, the wonderful aroma of food hit my nose from the dining car. Gravy, peas, and fish. Fresh fish I might add.

I followed my nose and my passion for eating. The Fourth class carriage was empty and I made a mental note that sleeping there was better than my horrible carriage. I then made my way past the chickens in Third class.

"Hello future dinners," I said, strolling past them.

They didn't like my humor. Three or four bunched up behind me.

I ran for the door. Not because I was afraid of a few chickens with claws reaching for me. As if I the Great Jack McCuddles, fears anything.

No, I ran because the smell of the fish was getting stronger from the next carriage.

Hunger does that to you, makes you run to the smell of food. Luckily, for the chickens the door wasn't locked. I jumped into the dining car and threw my back against the door. I am kind like that; I didn't want the chickens to wander loose around the train, as they might have gotten lost.

I saw McMoose sitting on the table eating his lunch. He was stuffing food into his greedy mouth. When he saw me, he smiled.

"Ahh, McStarving you found the dining car, I was beginning to wonder if you were going to join me for a spot of lunch," he said, after wiping some drool from his horrible mouth.

I jumped up on the chair across from him.

"Yes, I found it alright," I said. "Although the lock on my carriage door seems to be broken and delayed my arrival."

"Indeed, these old trains and their rusty locks, well now that you are here, you must try this fish. Waiter?"

He waved his paw around, feebly to get the waiter's attention. The dining car was completely empty. I got the impression that the chickens were the only other passengers on the train.

"Yes sir?" the waiter asked running over to our table.

"Some fish for my...friend," McMoose said.

I looked at the waiter with a tea towel draped over his arm and I thought there was something familiar about him. His white uniform was clean, his black hair was tidy and his face was round and kind. I think it was his yellow eyes, but I got distracted when he spoke.

"As I informed you, sir, when you ordered, that you were getting the last of the fish," he said sneering at me. "All we have left is gravy and peas."

"So you did, how terrible of me to forget and eat the last piece of fish," McMoose said. "Some gravy and peas then for good my friend."

"Very well sir," the familiar looking waiter said, before departing from our table.

My belly flopped and screamed in agony. The whole carriage smelled of fish. I could almost taste it. I wasn't going to survive on gravy and peas.

"How is your carriage?" McMoose asked me.

"Horrible."

"Good, good," he said ignoring my answer. He took a sheet of

15

paper from his pocket and started reading. "I have so many notes about this case to read before we arrive."

"Your dinner," the familiar waiter said, returning with a plate in his hands.

My eyes nearly fell out of my face. I saw three peas, swimming around the edges of the plate of gravy.

Slowly they made their way to the middle of the plate and when they had joined, each other, they parted company back towards the edge of the plate. I don't think they were real peas. As far as I know, peas are unable to perform synchronized dance routines in gravy.

"I think...there's something moving in my gravy," I said to the waiter.

"There can't be," he said. "You must be mistaken, sir. I have it on good authority that the chef drowned all the flies that were living in the fish."

"Well I suggest you look for yourself," I said raising the plate in my paws.

One of the peas hopped off the plate. It hung in the air and we eyeballed each other. The small black object made a beeline for my fur. I dropped the plate of gravy to the floor.

"Get it off me," I screamed.

I scratched my fur in a frantic attempt to remove whatever it was trying to make a home in my soft black fur. I felt it burrow under my fur. All it had left to do was send invites to its friends to the house warming party in my fur.

"Fleas," the waiter shouted. "The cat has fleas. Get it off the train before we are all infected."

McMoose jumped off the table and landed on the floor. The waiter hit me repeatedly with his tea towel. I rolled off the chair and hit the floor with a heavy thud. The waiter kept hitting me and McMoose just uselessly stood looking at me and checking his fur for fleas.

"Revenge is sweet," the waiter laughed and hit me again.

I had no idea what he was talking about. Why would anyone want to hurt me?

I am the cutest cat in the world and I never...oh wait...when Susie's back is turned, I do...not all the time...but I do a few evil spells, now and then.

Nothing terrible.

Maybe turn a kid's ice cream into worms or make a few snot monsters of out loud kids interrupting my naps. As I said, nothing terrible.

The tea towel hit me again.

"Stop hitting me," I cried.

I closed my eyes and protected my head with my paws. The tea towel ceased hitting me.

Suddenly I heard the train screech to a halt. I curled up into a little ball and passed out.

Not from fear, but from hunger. You see, I hadn't eaten in an hour.

Hunger can do that to you, make you pass out. I should carry snacks.

When I opened my eyes, McMoose was standing over me.

He was grinning.

I hate him. He is useless.

Chapter 3

"He's gone," McMoose said, "jumped off the train when it stopped. Did you know him?"

"What?" I muttered in shock.

"He pulled the emergency cord and jumped off the train."

"And what did you do?"

"I held the door open for him."

If I hadn't been in shock and starving I would have beaten that pesky mouse around the carriage.

"Did you know him?" McMoose asked me. "He shouted "snot monster" as he jumped."

I had turned so many kids into snot monsters over the years it was impossible for me to recall all of them. I don't see what the waiter's problem was, they always changed back into kids after a few hours.

Some even request that I make them into a snot monster so they can scare their teachers. Nobody wants hugs from a creature covered in snot and nose hair. Although, I have changed a few kids into snot monsters, just for fun, when Susie's back is turned. I was born to be evil after all.

"I have no idea who that was," I said jumping upright. "How long was I out?"

"About an hour. The conductor came around and said there will be no more food service now that the waiter is gone," McMoose said. "But I had such a big dinner. I won't need feeding till we get to Backwheretonowhere."

The gravy and two remaining dancing fleas on the floor didn't look very appetizing to me.

"But? My belly...empty...I need..."

"A nap is what I need," McMoose said holding his belly. "Well, I must leave you now and go back to my carriage. I will see you presently."

"And when is presently?" I somehow managed to ask.

"At two," he said taking his watch from his waistcoat.

Two o'clock was only an hour away. I felt a sigh of relief flow into my belly.

"Two o'clock then," I said, smiling and thinking of all the food I was going to eat.

"Have a nice night," McMoose said, heading for the door.

"What do you mean, nice night?"

"The train doesn't arrive at Backwheretonowhere till two," he said. "Did I not mention? My mistake...that's two o'clock...tomorrow afternoon."

"But that's a whole day away."

"So it is McWorries, you are indeed an intelligent cat...at times...I must get a good night's sleep, lots of work to do...after we walk to The Flea Palace of Delight."

"Walk?"

"Sorry did I not mention."

"No you didn't, there's a lot you aren't mentioning."

"I'm so excited with this mystery...my apologies McMoansalot. Yes, you see...the hotel is located outside the town."

"I gathered that," I said frowning. "But I suppose we can eat in the town before we leave for the hotel."

He shook his head, "Ghost town."

"Haunted?" I asked shivering.

I think the door of the train was still open and there was a draft coming in. That's the only thing that explained my shivering. It wasn't fear.

"Don't know about...ghosts," McMoose said. "I do know that it is desert...ed."

He had to mention something that sounded like food. My belly grumbled.

"Well till two," he said, leaving me alone in the carriage.

I heard the door lock behind him. But I tried it anyway. I was about to use a magic spell and unlock the door when the door flew open and knocked me on my backside.

"Tickets, all passengers must have a ticket," a dark figure said barging into the carriage.

I got up off my backside and scratched my ears.

He was a big round man, wearing a frilly white shirt, a blue waist jacket, matching breeches and stout buckle shoes. On the top of his head, he had a slouch felt hat. Under that grew long straggling red hair that flowed to his shoulders and a silver ring in his right ear.

He also had a long furry, braided, red beard. All he was missing was a patch over his eye to make him look like a pirate.

"Tickets?" he asked, squinting his right eye.

The right eye was blue and the left one was black. The left eye never moved. The closer I looked into his left eye the more I saw my own reflection. I hadn't seen how cute I looked in hours.

"I haven't all day, there be ports and rum that needs my attention," he sang.

"The mouse, McMoose has my ticket, I have no pockets," I said, shrugging my shoulders.

"A rat catcher does ye be?"

I was confused. "What is "yebe"?"

"Ye be fooling with me, laddie? I be the ticket inspector and conductor."

"Oh...I see...ye be...as in...you be...the..."

"I be what laddie?"

Not very clever I wanted to say.

"The mouse has my ticket," I said, instead.

"A funny rat catcher ye be, aye laddie, now what business do ye have on me ship?"

"Train," I said correcting him.

"Aye, that's what I said, laddie."

"No, you said ship."

"Aye laddie, be a fine ship. Now where be your ticket?"

How many times was I going to have to tell him McMoose had my ticket? I didn't answer him. I just shrugged my shoulders and smiled.

"Now see here laddie," he said, "a ticket for ye voyage ye need, or ye will walk the plank and be the food for the fishies if ye don't have a ticket."

Food...fish. I almost collapsed from hunger.

"Can't you ask the mouse for my ticket?"

"A stowaway you be. The rules of the ocean say ye shall scrub the decks or join the other stowaways sleeping in Davy Jones' locker."

I didn't correct him and tell him that a train travels over land and not the ocean. I had other things on my mind.

"Does Davy Jones' locker have warm blankets and food?"

"I like the cut of your jib," he said laughing. "I will get you a mop and bucket, ye can scrub the decks for your passage, we might even make a sailor of ye yet, me laddie."

I had to control my breathing. I got a hot flash before my fur tingled.

"You want me to...work?"

It hurt so much to say that word.

"That or swimming in Davy Jones' locker. What will it be laddie, the mop or the ocean?"

"Ocean," I said.

He started laughing.

"A funny one, a sense of humor is needed on these long sea voyages."

I wasn't trying to be funny. I wanted off this ship...I mean train.

I wanted food. I needed a nap and most of all I needed a mirror. I missed seeing my reflection. It loves me more than anything else does in the world and that includes selfish Susie. It's all her fault I am stuck here and about to be forced to...work.

"You can start in the last carriage...filthy there, that scurvy lot of a crew I have, they never bother cleaning that carriage," he said scratching his beard.

"But...my fur...get dusty...I haven't eaten...afternoon nap...I can't..."

"Aye, being a stowaway ye must be hungry, well ye must work first on me ship and then some food. We have some dried biscuits, not bad eating, but do take the time and pick weevils off them. Those little bugs will break your teeth if ye don't pick them off. I remember seeing one sailor lose his front tooth on one of them. Nasty business."

I started to choke. I started to shake. I shook my head and put on my sad eyes. No one can resist my green eyes when I am sad.

"Can't work," I whimpered. "Nap...no energy... need a nap."

My performance was award winning.

21

Who can resist such a cute cat like me?

Him. That's who.

He continued with his sickening story:

"Aye that's what he did, choked and choked, the little weevil was determined to set up home in his belly. Sick for weeks he was. Aye laddie, how we laughed when he went mad and jumped overboard."

"Why?"

"Because it was funny."

"Not why did you laugh. Why did he jump overboard?"

"Aye, he figured the sea water would make the weevil sick. Now enough of me sea stories, ye have cleaning to do, decks to be mopped."

I had to think quickly. "But...I haven't had any training; you know...knots and mops...too dangerous without proper work related training...and what will the pirate's union say when they find out you don't train your...pirates?"

He started laughing. I think he liked to laugh a lot.

"Make your way past them chickens and get yourself to the last carriage me laddie. Mopping is easy."

"But..."

"Aye and don't ye think ye can eat one of me chickens. I counted them myself before we sailed and I know how many there is."

I felt my whole body slump. I knew McMoose was tucked up in his bed with his stuffed belly, snoring peacefully. If I survived this trip, I was going to make him pay. I was done being nice and considerate to others.

My new employer waved at the door at the other end of the carriage and said:

"Off ye go laddie, but a wee word of advice. They say that the last carriage...It be haunted they say. Nothing can live there. Now I don't believe a word of it. One of me sailors did say he saw a ghost. Funny thing that...It was the last thing he ever said. Just quit. Jumped ship. Never saw him again. I don't believe it myself. The crew is a wee bit of a superstitious bunch if you ask me."

I wasn't asking him anything. Suddenly, I shivered.

I wished someone would seal up the drafts on this train.

Chapter 4

I opened the door to the next carriage that held the chicken. My eyes adjusted to the most horrible thing I had ever seen. The carriage was full of dead chickens.

They were lying all over the chairs with their heads hanging low. I was about to shout and tell the conductor that they were all dead till I heard one...make a rude noise from its behind. Its belly moved up and down and then it let off another...smelly one.

I crept slowly past the first one. The last thing I needed was a cranky chicken with a bad case of wind on my tail. Then I heard another...rude noise and then another and another. The room was starting to echo with the sound of releasing gas from chicken backsides.

The carriage smelled like rotten eggs. A yellow mist hung everywhere and stung my eyes. Tears streamed down my whiskers. I cupped my paw to my nose and ran for the door at the end of the carriage.

But I wasn't quiet or quick enough.

A chicken had awoken and attached itself to my back. It dug its claws into my back. I fell to the floor.

The chicken on my back started making chicken noises. I am not sure what they are called, maybe clucking, but it doesn't matter what the sound was, the chicken was pecking into my fur. That was the final straw.

My fur is too smooth and fluffy to have hideous bald spots. I wasn't about to take this from a future mayonnaise and lettuce sandwich.

I somehow moved it off my back. I threw my claws up at its hideous face and some feathers flew off into the air. The chicken looked shocked.

"Cluck, cluck," it...clucked.

I heard a huge rumbling noise and one mammoth release of wind from behind it. I knew it had just signaled all the other chickens to wake up. The smell nearly knocked me out. But I was brave and kept fighting the chicken.

With all my strength, I pushed it away from me. I ran for the door into Fourth class. I looked behind me as I opened the door and I swear I saw those chickens sharpening knives and putting napkins around their necks.

Okay, maybe I was hungry and hallucinating. But whatever I saw, I didn't wait to get a better look.

I entered the next carriage and threw my furry and very cute body against the door. I must have stayed pressed against that door for five minutes, sweating and listening to their clucking and sharpening of knives.

Finally, when their sounds had died down I headed for the Fifth class carriage. A ghost I could deal with, but hungry, maniacal chickens were off my menu. Actually, any chicken was now off the menu. That was a tough decision, given how hungry I was.

Hunger. It had been so long since my last meal, I couldn't even remember what I had eaten. I had to eat soon.

If I go past three hours without food...I might...it was too terrible to think of...but I might have to eat the dead woodlice in the corner of the carriage. I sat on the cold and damp carriage floor and watched the swinging light bulb.

This was no life for a cat as cute as me. I deserved better.

I was about to give up all hope when the door to my carriage opened. For the first time in my life, I was hoping to see McMoose.

But when the door opened the conductor walked in carrying a mop and bucket.

"Them chickens are odd, all they do is sleep," he said, placing the mop and bucket of water onto the floor.

"Sleep!" I said shocked.

"Aye laddie, they all be asleep back there," he said, nodding his head backward. "The fella I bought them off from the nuclear power plant said they were research chickens. Well, let me tell you, I haven't seen them research anything. They just eat and sleep."

Was this person an idiot? Research chickens, did he not know the meaning of the word research?

"Mop," he said, pointing at the mop on the floor.

"What about it?" I asked him.

"The floor," he laughed.

"Yes, I know, a floor, so?"

"Funny laddie, ye are funny. Now mop this here floor so I can see me reflection in it."

"If you want to see your reflection I can get you a mirror. Mirrors always announce their existence when I am near, they love my reflection...One day when I was a kitten...I was the cutest kitten in the world in case you didn't know...you should see the pictures...anyway this mirror actually..."

"Enough of your jokes me laddie. Scrub the decks."

"I'm a cat. I can't use a mop...I don't know how."

He just laughed and headed for the door.

"Watch out for the ghost," he said, closing the door as he left.

I wasn't afraid of a ghost. I was more afraid of...work. I grabbed the mop handle with two paws and stuck the stringy part of the mop into the bucket of water. It was heavy to lift out when covered in water. It made a splashing sound as it hit the floor, and so did I.

I got back up on my paws, heaved the mop back up from the floor, and tried again.

I did my best to push the soggy mop-head around the floor. A cat like me isn't used to such strenuous activity.

I even had to look up the word strenuous in a dictionary, as that's how hard the work was. Strenuous does sound better than backbreaking.

Yet, no matter where I mopped, the floor still looked dirty. My two paws hurt from holding the handle and my other two paws were soaking wet from the floor. I almost wanted to cry, but that would have made my face wet. And I am too cute to have a soggy face.

A magical cat like me should be doing evil, enough evil so I can pay someone else to mop the floor for me. Then I realized...magic.

I could cast a spell to clean the floor and have a nap. I knew I shouldn't and that it was wrong, but I was tired and very hungry. A cat like me can't think straight when I'm hungry and tired. Well, that was my defense if I was caught.

I steadied myself and was about to begin when suddenly I heard a voice call me.

"Cat?"

I looked around the dark room and the only thing I saw was the swinging light bulb. My hunger had gotten the best of me. I was hearing voices.

"Cat?" it said again.

I was going mad. I knew it.

My lack of naps and food was driving a wedge into my brain. I was losing my marbles, not that I have pockets for marbles, but you know what I mean.

Nevertheless, I had to do something to keep my sanity. You see, they don't allow mirrors in the Cat's Madhouse. I know because I saw a documentary once about the Cat's Madhouse. The cats run around on treadmills all day and do push-ups and lift weights.

One push-up would kill me and I can't live without my reflection. It is the only way I can see how cute I am. Oh, wait. Maybe that wasn't the Cat's Madhouse. However, it doesn't matter. I had to stop the voices in my head.

"I can't hear you," I said, mopping the floor.

"Cat. Who can't you hear?"

"Must be the wind," I said, keeping my eyes on the floor. "Just mopping the floor, can't hear a thing."

"Cat, who are you talking to?"

"The train engine goes choo-choo. No voices just the train engine going choo-choo."

"Choo-choo."

I whistled.

Darn voices in my head made me whistle like a train.

"Cat...," the voice said, slightly louder.

"Still, can't hear you."

Then the voices growled or was it my belly?

Anyway, I heard a growl. My fur began to shiver. I hated the drafts on this train. They were everywhere.

"You can't keep ignoring me," the voice said. "Cat, I know where there's food."

"Food, where? I mean choo-choo goes the engine...I'm not going mad...there are no voices in my head."

"Fresh pancakes with real maple syrup."

My mind was playing tricks on me. It had found my weakness. My belly rumbled. But if my brain did know the location of some pancakes, well who was I turn down a last meal before going to the Cat's Madhouse.

"Where?" I asked the voice.

"Where's what?"

"The pancakes...the pancakes...please I'm so hungry..."

"But first, you must help me."

"You're a voice in my head, how can you need help?"

"Cat...I need help. Stop this play acting and help me."

"Play acting, how dare you, I didn't imprison you in my head and I didn't invite you into my head. Be gone voice. I never want to hear you again...Oh wait...before you go...I'm starving, where are the pancakes you mentioned?"

"I am not in your head. I am the ghost of ships sailed-"

"But this is a train...so I am going mad. I knew it. I blame the three hours without food. What a terrible way for a cat like me to go, the cutest cat in the world...the cutest magical cat in the world...goes mad from hunger."

"Oh do stop moaning," the voice shouted at me. "Look down at the floor."

I did. It was true. You can see your reflection on a clean floor. I still looked cute, mad or not. I am so cute.

"Not at yourself, look over here, in the corner you idiot," the voice screamed.

I wasn't about to be fooled by a voice in my head, "Which corner?"

"Over here."

I gave in. I looked.

I saw the source of my madness staring back at me. It was hideous and beyond description.

Chapter 5

"A hamster," I screamed down at the tiny figure. "The voices living in my head belong to a hamster. I am Jack McCuddles and a cat like me does not have a hamster living in his brain."

"I'm not a voice in your head, more like a ghost," the tiny hamster said.

He didn't look like a ghost. He was a small brown furry hamster, wearing a t-shirt with black and white striped horizontal lines and small black breeches.

He really should have worn long trousers to cover his one hairy leg and the piece of wood attached to where his left leg should have been. It was only then that I noticed he also had a hook attached to where his left paw was missing.

"Allow me to introduce myself," he said, walking over to me. "My name is Count Von Nibbles, vampire hamster."

I looked at him funnily.

"I thought you said you were a ghost."

"Well...sure," he said, sniffing from his nose.

"Then how can you be a vampire?"

"It's a long story," he said.

"How long? I'm hungry and you promised me pancakes."

"I never made any such promise."

"Yes, you did."

"I said I knew where there are pancakes, not that I had any to give to you. Now please allow me to tell you my story, for I have much need of your help."

My belly rumbled.

"If you know where the pancakes are, you have to tell me."

"But first, you need to hear my story. I need your help."

"On an empty belly?"

"I've waited a long time to tell my story and now when I am so close to returning to my home, it needs to be told."

"Then five more minutes isn't going to make any difference and a good story always goes down better with food. Now if only we had some pancakes and-."

He lifted his hooked hand up to his mouth and spat on the hook and then he started wiping the hook on his breeches. I got his gross message.

"Please share your story with me," I said, smiling my cutest smile at him. But then again, all my smiles are cute, so it wasn't really much of an effort on my part.

"I have stowed away on this train," he said, looking at his hook, "so I can return home and save my family."

My empty belly wished he'd get to the point.

"I would begin at the beginning as it's always good to start at the start, but I haven't the time to start at the start," he said. "You see, I ran off to sea to stop an evil pirate. But, I think I have failed. He will make it to my family home beside the Flea Palace of Delight and I must stop him. Our home is in jeopardy because of him. Well, we think it's because of him. My wife didn't want me to go and find out the truth, she said it was dangerous but I didn't listen..."

He wasn't the only ones who didn't listen.

Talk about someone going on and on and saying absolutely nothing. I nodded my head at him and pretended to listen while I dreamed of pancakes, dripping with real maple syrup. I could almost taste them.

He kept talking. I kept eating my imagery pancakes and when I was finished with them, I looked at my reflection on the clean floor. I really looked extra cute today. I have no idea how I can possibly look extra cute, but I did.

"So can you help me and my family?" he asked me.

"What?" I asked looking at him.

"With what I just told you over the last five minutes. I know it was a lot to take in, but I have nobody else to ask for help."

I hadn't realized he'd finished his story or that five minutes had passed. It is amazing how time flies when you look at something as cute as me.

I took one long look at his hook. It was shiny. My green eyes looked especially radiant reflected off his hook.

"You will have all the pancakes you can eat once my family is safe, that much I can promise you," he said, extending his right paw to me. "Do we have a deal?"

All the pancakes I can eat. I didn't hesitate to shake his paw. It felt cold and hairy.

"Of course, we have a deal," I said, "although can I have some of those pancakes...like as a deposit? You know half up front now and half when I do what it is you said I need to do."

"When the time is right, I will re-appear," he said, gripping my paw. "I trust you followed everything I said, it's vital you fully understand what I need from you."

"I have a few questions," I said.

I wasn't lying.

I had many questions for him. I had no idea what he was talking about, well aside from the mention of pancakes.

"No time McCuddles, I must conserve my energy," he said. "I trust you McCuddles, don't let me or my family down. You know the terrible price we will all pay if you fail."

"We...me...what price?"

But my question went unanswered.

He disappeared into a puff of smoke that smelt like burnt bacon. My belly started to hurt. Burnt bacon would taste lovely with some pancakes. I needed food.

The door to the carriage opened behind me and the conductor stepped inside with a tray in his arms.

"The floor looks ship-shape, laddie. Well done. I brought you some biscuits," he said placing the tray on the ground beside me.

I stared hungrily at the tray. The biscuits were dark brown with even darker and browner big chocolate chips on them.

"I'm starving," I said.

"Eat away, laddie, ye deserve them," he said, heading back to the door, "and now if you will excuse me, I have some ship's business to take care of."

I heard the bolt lock on the door. I was all alone in my dark and damp carriage. At least I had food.

I picked up one of the biscuits and bit into it. My tooth nearly broke on the large piece of chocolate chip on the biscuit.

I picked one of the chocolate chips off the biscuit with my claws and was about to place it into my mouth when it moved. No, not my mouth, the chocolate chip moved.

It crawled across my paw. I threw it on the floor and was nearly sick.

"Weevils," I screamed at it.

My fur went all spiky. I must have looked horrible with spiky fur, but I wasn't about to let that ruin my dinner. I picked all the weevils off the biscuits and flung them into the corner of the carriage. I don't think they were too happy about that.

A small team of weevils crawled back over to the tray to reclaim their home on my biscuits. But I wasn't about to share with them.

I stuffed all the biscuits into my mouth and swallowed them as quickly as I could. They didn't taste very nice, but that was the least of my problems.

I now had an army of weevils seeking vengeance.

One of them jumped onto my back. I had only just shaken him off my fur when another jumped onto me and then another.

I rolled around on the floor trying to squash them, but it was useless. There was too many. I had no choice.

I jumped into the mop bucket full of dirty water. It was horrible, the water smelled of rotting sweaty socks. I splashed around trying to get the weevils off my fur. Some of the water went in my mouth and into my ears. Luckily, for me, I also felt some of the weevils letting go of my fur. I jumped back out and onto the floor.

I was weevil free. I shook myself a few times to make sure and I spat a lot to get the taste of the dirty water from my mouth. I peeked inside the bucket and saw the weevils swimming around and drinking the dirty water. The funny thing is, I think they were happy inside the mop bucket.

I wasn't so happy. I was drenched and filthy. I crawled over to the corner and started grooming myself. The water tasted horrible. I was cold and damp.

This was truly the worst day of my life. I didn't deserve any of this. I was cold and alone, hunched up in the corner and feeling very miserable when I heard a clucking noise outside the door.

The noise got louder and then I heard the bolt open on the door. I ran to the far end of the carriage and watched five chickens stroll casually, inside the carriage. Each one had a fork tucked under their wings and a napkin wrapped around their throats.

I knew someone must have let them in. There is no way a chicken can open a door. On the other hand, I am a cat and I can open a door. Anyway, I wasn't about to ask them, because whoever had let them in, didn't close the door behind them.

I had an exit.

I summoned up every ounce of courage I had and ran with my two claws extended for the open door. A fork ripped into my sides and lifted me into the air.

I looked down at the smiling chicken that had me impaled on its fork. The chicken's beak was readying itself for my swinging legs. I was about to be cat soup.

I heard a voice scream my name, wrongly. It was McMoose.

"McNuggetity, can you stop playing with the chickens for a moment, it's time to go to work," he said, from the open doorway.

The chicken dropped me and removed its fork from my belly. The chicken then just started pecking around the floor, all casually, as if it was a normal chicken.

"The chickens," I shouted, "McMoose the chickens they are possessed."

"Actually, I think they are free range chickens," he shouted back.

"I said possessed not processed..."

"You are always thinking about food, now come on we have arrived at Backwheretonowhere."

I walked slowly past the chickens. Each one eyeballed me as I went past them. I didn't return their stares.

I kept my eyes ahead and on McMoose. As much as I hate him, I was glad to see him. Even if I did suspect he had let the chickens in to scare me.

"Your carriage is very clean," he said, looking at the floor.

I wanted to knock his bowler hat off his head and kick him up the...But I didn't.

"The train seems to have arrived early," Mc Moose said. "How very fortunate for us as we now have more time to work on the mystery."

The train had arrived early. I had never heard of a train arriving early. Something was amiss and I am never wrong. Well, almost never wrong. I can be modest...occasionally.

"McMoose, exactly what is the mystery?" I asked him.

"To find out why the hotel has no guests and to find the vampire that has bitten the few they have had."

I didn't care one bit.

I was cold, hungry and had been mistreated all day. It was time to set this mouse straight and tell him I was going home.

"Look, McMoose...Charlie...I...well it's like this..."

He waved his umbrella at me and said, "If we hurry, I am sure we can get some food at the station."

That changed everything. "Let's go," I said. "We have a mystery to solve."

Chapter 6

I jumped off the train and felt a cold fog dampen my fur. The lights around the train platform did nothing to help me see past my whiskers on my cute face.

"Come on McFoggles, this way," McMoose said, walking into the train station. "Did you eat?" he called back to me.

"Not really, unless you count some dried crumbs that once were biscuits," I said, to the back of his bowler hat.

"Biscuits, good that should keep you going, no need to stop for food," he said, stopping beside three suitcases. "Suitcases...McCudldles."

He is a great detective to have worked out that they were suitcases.

"Yes, I believe you are correct, they are suitcases," I said, looking closely at the small suitcases.

"My suitcases," he said, pointing with his umbrella.

He is not just a great detective; he is a master detective to recognize his own suitcases. "Well observed McMoose, no criminal will get anything past you."

"McCuddles, enough of your joking, now carry them."

"What? Why?"

"How else will you earn your pay?"

"I get paid?"

"Well no, you see Susie gets your wages, now carry the suitcases for me, a sleuth cannot be seen carrying his luggage."

"I thought I was hired as a detective. Wait, what do you mean Susie gets my wages?"

I don't think he heard me.

"Suitcases McCudddles," he said, leaving the train station.

I picked up two of the suitcases in my paws and chomped down on the third one with my teeth. The suitcase tasted plastic, all the better, for what I had planned for his suitcase.

My teeth punctured some small holes into the suitcase. By the time, we get to wherever we are going; his suitcase will be full of my saliva. Usually, I don't like drooling, but I can make exceptions, for special cases, like this one.

I followed him outside and into the thick fog.

There wasn't a sound to be heard till his little voice squeaked, "This way."

"You sure?" I mumbled through his suitcase.

"Absolutely."

We walked for over an hour in the fog before he spoke to me again. He stopped walking, removed his bowler hat, and wiped his furry head.

"This is indeed a mystery," he said, "the hotel should be here."

I spat out his suitcase.

"Maybe they moved," I said.

He gave me a long hard stare. I stared back. I look cute when I stare.

"Back to the station," he grumbled.

"What? But I'm tired and hungry and these suitcases are heavy."

"Something foul is afoot."

"Chicken?"

"I said foul, not fowl. I think we have been tricked and someone does not want us to make it to our destination."

Picking up the suitcases, I put the half-eaten suitcase in my paw and put a fresh one into my mouth, and kicked the remaining suitcase along the road with my leg. He was too busy sleuthing his way back to the train station to notice.

Somehow, it took us two hours to find our way back. McMoose blamed the fog for slowing us down. I got the impression we had walked around in circles, but I was too tired to argue.

We both collapsed into the station's waiting room under the feet of the stationmaster. He was wearing a peaked navy cap that matched his suit. His brown eyes looked tired but I think he was more shocked to see the cutest cat in the world carrying suitcases.

"You can't sleep here," he said greeting us.

It wasn't much of a greeting. I left McMoose to his sleuthing. I was too tired and hungry.

"I say, this is the Backwheretonowhere?" McMoose asked the stationmaster.

"No, this is the Nextonowhere station," he answered.

Typical, McMoose had gotten us lost. I told you he wasn't much of a sleuth.

"Great," I said, with a hint of sarcasm, "so we are stuck in the middle of nowhere."

"No, the Middleofnowhere station is up the road from here," the stationmaster said.

"But our train stopped here," McMoose said. "It was a big steam train and the conductor let us off here."

"Do they still use steam trains? Not that it matters, no trains ever stop here."

"Then why do you have a train station here?"

"Well just in case one does want to stop."

I saw McMoose's shoulders slump and his head follow. He removed his bowler hat and scratched his puny head. I would have laughed but I was too hungry.

"How do we get to Backwheretonowhere?" he asked the stationmaster.

"If you have a bus ticket, you can take a bus."

"Great," McMoose said smiling, "can I have two tickets?"

"No, you can't."

"But you said we could take the bus."

"Of course, you can take the bus, as long as you have a ticket, anyone with a ticket can take the bus."

"Great," McMoose said. "Then...can I please have...two tickets...please?"

"This is a train station, we don't sell bus tickets here, but I can sell you a train ticket."

McMoose looked at the stationmaster and then he glanced over at me. He looked confused. I don't know why he was looking at me. I'm just the baggage carrier and not the great sleuth.

McMoose returned his confused gaze back to the stationmaster and asked him, very slowly, "Where...is the...bus station?"

"Let me think," the stationmaster said. "You want the

Backwheretonowhere bus station?"

"No, Backwheretonowhere is where we want to go," McMoose
answered.

"Lucky for you then as that's where the bus station is. And now if
you don't mind, it's time to lock up the train station for the night and you
can't sleep here."

I jumped to my feet. "I need food. Can we get dinner in town?"

"They serve breakfast, lunch and dinner in the restaurant," the
stationmaster answered cheerfully.

"Phew," I gasped. "I'm starving, where is the restaurant?"

"Top of the town, but there's no point going there now," the
stationmaster said, shaking his head.

I didn't want to ask. But I had to know.

"Why is there no point in going there?"

"The restaurant closes at six," he answered.

"But that's dinner time," I cried.

"In some parts of the world it might be, but not around here."

"At least there must be a hotel we can sleep in?" a deflated
McMoose asked him.

"Yes, if you've reserved a room, have you reserved a room?"

"No," McMoose cried.

"Not to worry, I am sure they have a free room," he said,
smiling. "Business is bad, so I believe they have lots of free rooms."

"Great," I said. "And where is your fine hotel located."

"Funny you should ask me that, the Flea Palace of Delight is in
the Backwheretonowhere. Now isn't that funny, why that's the town you
are both looking for."

It wasn't funny. Nor was the cold damp fog we both found
ourselves back walking blindly in looking for the Backwheretonowhere.
I looked at McMoose and the only thing that stopped me from hitting
him was my tiredness, my hunger, and his stupid suitcases.

"I think there's a conspiracy afoot to stop us from getting to the
Flea Palace of Delight," he announced to the fog.

I was too annoyed to ask him what the big word "conspiracy"
meant or why he was talking to the fog. I think the idiot got off at the
wrong station and was making up excuses and big words.

Instead, I asked him, "Which way?"

"This way," he motioned in the fog.

I dug my teeth into the hole free suitcase and followed him for hours. My paws hurt, my belly hurt and the damp fog was making my fur all matted. The only thing that kept me going was the thoughts of pancakes and a warm bed.

His bags became heavier and heavier. The temptation was building to drop one of his suitcases on the ground. But every few seconds he would look back at me.

I knew he was counting his suitcases.

Finally, we saw a blinking light cutting through the fog and the sound of a foghorn. I think I smelled fish. Food was close.

"That must be the lighthouse," McMoose happily announced.

"What gave it away?" I muttered.

"The hotel shouldn't be much further."

I heard water hitting the edge of a cliff. Yes, I did wish he would follow that sound in the thick fog.

He didn't. We both saw some light emitting from the windows of the hotel ahead of us and walked in that direction instead.

The closer we got to the building the more my belly rumbled and the more my paws begged for a warm bed. McMoose walked up the steps of the hotel and entered the glass revolving door first.

He must have pushed hard on the glass before he jumped out as I entered the next empty enclosure. The doors kept spinning around and I couldn't stop them or find a gap to squeeze through.

I was trapped and getting dizzy. Around and around I spun.

"McCuddles stop playing with the doors and get in here," McMoose ordered me, from inside the warm and snug hotel foyer.

"I can't," I shouted, dropping his suitcase from my mouth.

"Be careful with my suitcase," he gasped.

Everything was becoming a blur of lights and shadows. I heard his voice shouting for me to jump through the gap. But there was no gap.

Around and around I kept going and getting dizzier and dizzier with each turn. If I had anything in my belly, it would have splattered onto the glass.

The world was a blur and I kept turning. Hunger and tiredness had me on my knees. I held my stomach. My lights went out.

Chapter 7

When I woke up, I felt a really warm and soft pillow under my head. I needed that pillow, as my head was thumping sore. A nice velvet blanket was covering my fur. It was fluffy, almost as fluffy as my fur, but nothing is as fluffy as my fur, that is why I said, almost.

I opened my eyes and tried to focus on my surroundings. All I saw was McMoose looking down at me.

He looked angry. But it is hard to tell when you are as ugly as he is. However, his lips were moving. I didn't want to hear his voice but I had no control over my ears or his volume.

"McBuggles, you disgraced me in front of my clients with your play acting. I had to carry my own bags and you up to this room."

"Room spinning...food?" I whispered.

"Stop acting and get up, we have work to do."

Not a chance, the pillow was too nice to leave.

"Room spinning...hunger...must eat...to stop the spinning."

"Lord McBedbugs wishes to discuss the case with us over breakfast," McMoose said, pulling on the lapels of his waistcoat before straightening his tie with his tiny paws.

"Breakfast," I cried. "What are we waiting for?"

My belly needed food.

I pulled the fluffy blanket off my even more fluffy fur and stood up. The bed was huge. It was that big that if I stayed a week I would still find a new space to curl up and sleep on each naptime.

I was at the door before I even realized I should have asked about room service. But then again I didn't want to get crumbs in my bed.

I jumped up and clung to the handle of the door and swung backward to open it. People underestimate how difficult it is to open a door when you are a cat. They really should lower door handles.

"Come on McMoose, we have a mystery to solve," I shouted before swinging into the hallway.

My paws landed on the carpet. It was an expensive carpet. Every step was massaging my paws with its fluffy material. It was a lovely feeling. I was going to like staying in this hotel.

McMoose followed me down the stairs while I followed my nose to the smell of food. Actually, it was the smell of burnt toast, but I was that hungry I didn't care.

We passed the empty reception desk in the foyer surrounded by huge paintings of stuff I couldn't care less about. The area would have looked nicer with a painting of me on the walls, but even the most talented artist can never capture my true beauty.

I entered the dining room and saw a few patches on the walls where some paintings had once hung on hideous flowery wallpaper. The room had ten tables, all set for breakfast, but with no guests around them. That meant only one thing.

More food for me. I jumped onto the seat at the table beside the window and admired my reflection in the glass.

"Something is amiss with this hotel," McMoose said, climbing onto a chair.

I broke off staring at my reflection to look at McMoose. It wasn't easy, yet somehow I managed to look at away from my beauty.

He huffed and puffed climbing up and onto the table. I know I could have easily lifted him up, but it was more fun to watch him struggle.

"What is amiss?" I asked him.

"The lack of guests...The missing paintings on the walls...The plastic forks on the table," he said.

"Plastic forks," I gasped. "How will I see my reflection when I'm eating? I suppose I could eat and look out the window."

"And what do you see out the window?"

"My reflection."

"No you idiot, what do you see regarding the hotel grounds?"

I looked past my reflection, even hungry I looked cute.

"The gardens...look at the gardens," he ordered me. "Tell me what you observe?"

"A few dead trees, some flower beds with no flowers, a few large holes that need filling in. So?"

"They are clues McCuddles."

"You are right McMoose...lots of clues..." I said. I began to put the parts of the jigsaw together in my head. "They need a gardener, case solved and on an empty stomach," I proudly said.

"No McIdiot...you are missing the clues around you."

"Look I have a name...and I find it upsetting-"

Suddenly a voice called out, "What would you like for breakfast?"

"Pancakes with real maple syrup," I instinctively called back.

I looked over at the door and saw an old looking bald man walking towards us. He was tall and skinny and wearing a badly creased brown suit and furry brown slippers.

"Lord McBedbugs," the over eager mouse announced, "allow me to introduce myself, my name is McMoose...Charles...McMoose...The sleuth."

I almost laughed at the way he said Charles, but I had more worrying concerns. I was afraid my order hadn't been heard.

"Pancakes with real maple syrup," I said.

"We have toast and marmalade for breakfast," Lord McBedbugs said.

"That would be satisfactory," Charles McMoose...the sleuth, said.

"But I ordered pancakes," I cried.

Then Lord McBedbugs did the most unthinkable thing I had ever seen. He pulled out a chair and took a seat at our table, without firstly going to the kitchen for my food.

I was shocked. I began to shake.

Nobody noticed my distress.

I tried again. "Breakfast?" I asked.

Lord McBedbugs looked seriously at McMoose.

"Please, tell me what has happened?" McMoose asked him. "Hold back on no detail, no matter how trivial or slight it may seem to you, it may be a huge clue to my expert ears."

His what! His expert ears. Did his expert ears not hear my cry for food?

"It all began a month ago," Lord McBedbugs began. "I suspected someone was driving off all our guests and stopping them from getting here, at first we didn't know why..."

"Because of poor customer service I would imagine," I added.

I looked to see if he had a walkie-talkie or something on him to call the kitchen with to order our food. He didn't. He just kept moaning on about his problems.

"Our business died overnight," he said.

So did all his customers, from lack of food.

He continued:

"I had to sell all the silverware, the paintings and all the antique mirrors to pay the rent and bills. We can't even afford to buy food now."

"What?" I shuddered, "you have no...mirrors...or...food?"

"We have toast and marmalade," he said smiling at me.

My belly was stilling waiting for proof on that one.

McMoose gave me a long hard stare. My belly returned with a long, loud rumble.

"I have a theory," continued Lord McBedbugs, as if my hunger cared if he continued with his moans, "I think it has something to do with the vampire hamsters in the lighthouse."

"Like the ghost, I met on the train," I gasped.

"He said vampires, not ghosts," McMoose said, waving his paw at me to be quite, "please go on Lord McBedbugs, you were saying...the vampire hamsters?"

"They run the lighthouse, hard workers that spend the whole night on their hamster wheels connected to a dynamo to make the lights work."

"And why do you think they are involved?" McMoose asked him.

If he was any good of a sleuth, he would ask questions that are more important. Such as, where is my toast?

"They keep to themselves and have no contact with us, they are great landlords, leave us to run the hotel for them," Lord McBedbugs said, "they live in the lighthouse past the cliff, you can take a boat over to them."

"We can...after breakfast," I hinted.

"And why do you think they are involved?" McMoose asked

42

him, again.

"And where is breakfast?" I quickly asked.

"Breakfast, oh dear me, yes breakfast," he said, rising from his chair.

Finally, I was going to be fed, or so I believed.

McMoose put out his arm and waved down at Lord McBedbugs' seat, "Lord McBedbugs, you still haven't answered my question."

"What question was that?"

"Why do you think they are involved?"

I wanted to cry the moment Lord McBedbugs sat back down. I was never going to get food. I hadn't had a proper meal in days, weeks, I forget. I was wasting away. Any longer and my fur would wilt. I needed feeding. Now. It was too much for me all this back and forth and false promises of food.

"Food," Lord McBedbugs said.

"Need..." I said, shaking my paw in the air, "feeding."

"Precisely," Lord McBedbugs exclaimed. "That is one intelligent cat, he is absolutely right."

Well, of course, I was right about whatever he thought I was right about. I am the cutest and smartest cat in the world.

I am never wrong.

"What was I right about?" I asked Lord McBedbugs.

"Feeding...guests," he replied.

I smiled. "Yes, you should always feed-"

"No-"

"What do you mean no?" I cried. "I need feeding."

Lord McBedbugs placed his hands on his face and cried, "The vampire hamsters, they started feeding...on..."

McMoose leaned closer to him and asked, "On?"

It seemed a good time to remind him that I was still hungry and that I had my needs. "Toast," I suggested.

He pulled his hands off his face and stared at me. I didn't like the way his blue eyeballs wavered.

With a long gasp of air, he said, "They began to feed...on...my guests."

I had a bad feeling that I wasn't going to get my toast when McMoose fell on his backside from shock and shouted, "McCuddles, we must go to the lighthouse straight away and investigate this matter."

I had to stop the eager mouse before we became toast.

"Now wait a second," I said. "We need to make a plan...over breakfast."

However, I was too late. McMoose was on his feet eager to leave and then the most dreadful sound filled up the dining room from speakers hidden in the ceiling:

"The kitchen is now closed, thank you for dining with us this morning. See you for lunch at noon."

McMoose was already on the floor with his umbrella pointing to the outdoors. I knew I wasn't going to get any breakfast. He ran. I followed.

He stepped inside the revolving doors.

"Come on McCuddles, we have vampires to catch," McMoose shouted.

I looked at the revolving door and pushed with all my strength. He went spinning. I sat back and watched him swirl around past me.

I left by the dining room window.

I wasn't in much of a hurry to meet vampire hamsters.

Chapter 8

I found McMoose on the steps of the hotel examining the empty holes and filled in patches scattered randomly around the front garden. Seeing the hotel in daylight without any fog was intimidating.

The building was huge, five floors in all with lots of sash windows. I think the design was...well I have no idea. I have no interest in books about homes and gardens because I am never featured in them.

"Do you see the pattern?" McMoose asked me.

I took my eyes away from the building and looked around at the random patches in the garden.

"Yes," I lied.

"Very odd, it's like someone was looking for something."

"Just what I was thinking," I lied, again.

It was holes in a garden, probably gophers or mole or whatever they are called.

He walked onto the damp grass and beckoned me to follow with his umbrella. I wanted to grab that umbrella and knock his bowler hat off. But the empty holes only reminded me of my hunger.

A cat like me, should under no circumstances, go without food. I knew I was going to have to have stern words with Susie when I saw her next. How dare she abandon me with this fool and allow me to go hungry. I was put on this planet to be obeyed and adorned. Not to follow a mouse on an empty belly.

"A compass," McMoose said, scratching his chin.

"Are you lost?" I asked him.

"No McMuddles, a compass, each hole indicates the direction on a compass," he said, gesturing to one of the holes. "See we have north up there, you are south and there is east and west."

"So?"

"Each hole is exactly the same distance from the middle, and you know what that means?"

"Yes I do," I said and of course, I was lying. "I do believe you may have solved this complex case, and rather easily, but that's not surprising given your mighty intellect. But McMoose, I really must insist you rest your powerful brain and perhaps set aside all other business till after lunch."

"There is only one way to find out if I am...right, we must speak to the other party involved in this...mystery."

I shivered, but only because the early morning breeze had a bite in it.

"The vampire hamsters?" I asked him.

"Indeed and there's no time like the present. Come on McSurly to the lighthouse, the sea air will help us work up an appetite for lunch."

I didn't need help to work up an appetite. I was already starving. I hate him.

I followed McMoose to the back of the hotel to the sight of a sheer drop over the cliff edge.

Yes, I know what you are thinking.

I didn't. I barely had the energy to walk let alone push him off the cliff.

From the cliff edge, we saw a small concrete path, swirling down to the beach. About a mile out to sea was the lighthouse. Although you will have to trust me on that. I am a cat and have no idea how far a mile actually is. The lighthouse was a drab gray monstrosity of a building with a small island around it.

It didn't look very inviting. That didn't stop McMoose. His tiny feet sped up.

As we walked down the steps built into the cliff, I did have the temptation to trip McMoose. That would have been a silly thing to do. Not because he might get hurt. The ambulance might take hours to arrive and I feared missing lunch and eating hospital food. Yuck.

We made it to the beach without incident and we found the small rowing boat tied to a log on the beach.

"Untie the boat," McMoose said, jumping into the boat.

I did as he said and jumped in beside him. The boat didn't move.

"You need to push us into the water McCuddles," McMoose said leaning back.

"But I'll get wet."

"The sooner we are in the water the quicker we will get to our destination and then back in time for lunch."

I hopped out and started pushing. My only motivation was the hope the vampire hamsters weren't home and had left some food behind.

My arms screamed in pain as I pushed the boat across the sand. Once I felt my legs get wet from the icy cold water, I jumped back into the rowing boat.

"Paddles," McMoose said.

"Only dogs paddle, I'm a cat, we don't like water so I'm not paddling anywhere. I'm staying on this boat and you can't do anything about it."

"No McCuddles, you have mistaken what I said, the paddles, you will need them to row us to the lighthouse."

I looked around the rowing boat and didn't see any.

"Where are they?" I asked him.

"On the beach, you'd better swim back and get them before we drift out to sea."

My paws became claws.

"Hurry now," he said, smiling at me, "we don't want to be late for lunch."

The icy cold bit into my fur when I hit the water. Luckily, the water was only knee deep. I grabbed the paddles and made my way back into the boat.

"Good chap, McCuddles," he cheered, "the sea breeze will dry you off. Now put your back into it, the current is strong and I don't fancy seagulls for lunch."

He opened his umbrella and positioned it over his head. "Try not to splash too much; I would prefer to arrive at the lighthouse dry."

He didn't say alive.

I rowed the boat towards the ever-increasing lighthouse, never once complaining to McMoose. I was too tired and hungry to say anything and whenever I did try to open my mouth, the seawater splashed into it.

Finally, we hit the beach surrounding the lighthouse. I jumped out and dragged the boat onto the sand and pebbles. It was times like these I wished I had shoes. The peddles on the beach were digging into

47

my paws. I ran across them as quickly as I could to the soft grass on the hill that led up to the lighthouse.

"Nice to see you so eager," McMoose said joining me. "Shall we?"

"Shall we what?"

"Call on the vampire hamsters."

"But it's daytime, vampires sleep during the day. So do we really need to wake them up?"

"Yes McCuddles, if I'm correct about those holes in the hotel's garden, then yes, the vampire hamsters hold the key."

The air around the lighthouse got colder. I didn't shiver. I shuddered.

McMoose had a smug look on his face. There was no stopping him. He, in his puny mind, had solved the mystery. A mystery that I might add wasn't a mystery.

A lazy gardener digs a few holes and quits his job, probably because the hotel doesn't give him any lunch. And as for the lack of guest, well what do they expect when they don't feed them. There was no mystery here. It was silly to bother the vampire hamsters over nothing.

"The lighthouse looks empty," I said. "Perhaps we should turn back."

"No way McCuddles. Come on you need to earn your wage."

McMoose led the way, as usual, to the front door of the lighthouse.

The door had flaky blue paint on it and a few scratches beside the bell. He pointed at the bell. I hate being his assistant. I pressed the bell and waited.

I knew that who or whatever was about to open the door had just gotten a delivery of fresh and warm flowing blood. Therefore, I stepped back and allowed McMoose to stand forward to be greeted first.

He was in charge and should have that privilege. It had nothing to do with fear.

The door began to squeak open. Darkness spilled out from the cracks of the door. We were about to meet a blood hungry vampire hamster.

I was doomed. I had nowhere to run and after all that rowing on an empty belly, I had no energy left in me to run.

This was it, as far as I was concerned, the end. No more cutest cat in the world. I'd be missed, my beauty, denied to millions, a terrible tragedy. A river of tears shed in my honor, flooding the hearts of my many admirers. The sorrow they will feel, the pain, this is not how it should be.

And the songs, how many songs will be written about my beauty?

Perhaps millions that I'd never hear. And the mirrors, they will feel it the worst, so many...denied to ever grace my reflection.

Without me, they will be useless and under the strain, they will crack. The world was about to get seven years of bad luck. All because of a stupid mouse.

A mouse whose last words will ring in my ears:

"I say, is this the home of the vampire hamsters?"

Chapter 9

A tiny brown hamster in a black dress stood looking at McMoose and then cast her angry eyes at me. I took in a deep breath and waited for the fangs to appear.

"What? I'm busy," she shouted.

"I do beg your pardon," McMoose began, "I am in need of your help...about the hotel... Miss...Ms.?"

"Countess Von Nibbles," she said. "Oh the sun, I do hate the sun, come inside quickly before I am turned into toast."

McMoose went first. I hesitated, but a strong smell of steaming fish hit my nose. I jumped in beside him. She closed the door behind me.

The hallway was dark and small. A large metal staircase extended upwards, with a small trapdoor at the bottom of the staircase. I didn't give the trapdoor much thought because the fish smelled almost done.

"Smells nice, are you preparing lunch?" I asked her.

"Yes," she replied. "Now what can I do for you both."

McMoose extended his paw to her and said, "My name is McMoose...Charles...McMoose the sleuth, pleased to meet you."

"A what?"

"Sleuth," he replied.

"Fancy name for a detective, so what do you want?"

This was the second time he hadn't introduced me. I wasn't happy about that. He had ignored me when we met McBedbugs and now, with food cooking and the chance of a meal, I wasn't going to be forgotten.

"My name is McCuddles...Jack McCuddles...umm...also a sleuth," I said, extending my paw to her.

"My assistant," McMoose said, correcting me.

"Assistant sleuth," I said, smiling at her.

McMoose shook his head at me, "No, you're the assistant to the sleuth."

"If I assist the sleuth then I'm the assistant sleuth, just like the person that assists a chef is called the assistant chef."

"The person who washes the dishes also assists the chef by providing clean plates, but they aren't called an assistant chef, they are called the dishwasher."

"Are you two done? My lunch is boiling away to nothing," Countess Von Nibbles said.

"Smells divine, I'm not one to refuse food," I said.

"I wasn't offering, so you won't have to start refusing," she said. "Now can we get on with this?"

"Why yes, the hotel has had a drop in business and you are accused of...feeding off the guests...What do you say to this?" McMoose said, tapping his umbrella on the floor.

"To a tapping umbrella? I have nothing to say to a tapping umbrella."

"Not to my tapping, to my accusation...of feeding."

"I didn't offer the cat any food, so don't accuse me of feeding him. To be honest he looks like he needs a diet."

"I haven't eaten in days, not since the crumbs I got after that stupid ghost-vampire hamster disappeared from the train," I screamed. "And I do not need to diet."

McMoose glared at me. "What vampire hamster?"

"Count Yon, Ron...something or other."

"Count Von Nibbles?" she gasped.

"Now that you say it...maybe, yes."

"Small like me with brown hair," she said.

"Yes, with a hook on his left-"

"Oh my...no," she cried, "he lost his paw, he loved that paw."

I tried to console her.

"He was fine. It kind of matched his wooden leg, made him look all pirate-ly"

"His leg as well," she cried. "Not his left leg, please not the left one, he always favored his left leg when playing football."

I found it hard to imagine a vampire hamster playing football. Therefore, I tried to console her again.

"Well, I'm sure now the ball will only pass through his body as ghosts don't have a solid form."

For some reason, she fell onto her knees and started crying, loudly.

"He's dead," she hollered, "Dead, my husband is dead."

I was worried. All this crying was leaving the steamed fish unattended.

It is never a good idea to leave cooking food unattended. If she was usually this unconcerned with their lunch, I was starting to see why her husband had run off to sea to become a pirate.

I had to do something to help.

"But you're a vampire, that means you're dead anyway, so I'm sure he's fine, but your fish, well, that may need some help. Do you want me to run upstairs and keep an eye on it?"

"You monster," she cried.

"No, I'm a cat, the cutest cat in the world, not a monster. Monsters are big scary creatures. I can't imagine how you can mistake the two."

McMoose was still glaring at me. He is not much use in an emergency.

"The lunch," I said loudly to him, hoping to wake him up, "we have to save the lunch."

McMoose was still standing around looking all, glaring and useless. I ran for the metal stairs. Someone had to save lunch.

I took each step two at a time. It was an effort, but overcooked fish isn't very nice.

I was sure that when she calmed down and saw how I had saved dinner that she would offer us some. I finally made it to the source of the alluring smell. I pushed the door open and looked around for the cooker.

I spotted the steaming pot and was about to rescue the fish when something grabbed my leg. I looked down and saw an even tinier brown hamster hanging off my leg. I shoved hard but the hamster had its teeth deep into my flesh.

Hunger was in its eyes.

"Stop biting me," I cried, "I'm here to save lunch."

It didn't let go.

Suddenly I heard Countess Von Nibbles shout from the kitchen door, "Let go of him you monster."

"Yes," I shouted at the biting hamster, "let go of me."

Countess Von Nibbles screamed at me, "I meant you cat, let go of my son."

"But he's the one biting me," I screamed back at her.

"Oh, no," McMoose screamed.

"Why is everyone screaming," another small brown hamster screamed. "What's that cat doing to my brother?"

I had no idea where she came from, and I didn't care. The hamster biting my leg let go and ran off towards his sister.

Everything went quiet for a few seconds. Until McMoose screamed:

"Susie is going to kill me."

I looked over at him and saw his eyes looking at my leg. I followed his eyeballs and saw a small tuft of my fur was missing and two tiny bite marks.

It was nothing. I still looked cute and it didn't really distract from my beauty.

"It's nothing. A piece of steamed fish will make me forget all about it," I said to McMoose.

"You don't understand," Countess Von Nibbles said.

I smiled at her and said, "A small piece of fish would be fine. I can share, this one time."

She addressed the hamster that had bitten me, "Frank, what did you do?"

"Sorry mom, I heard you say monster and then this ugly thing came barging into the room," he replied.

"How dare you call me ugly, I will have you know I'm the cu-"

"McCuddles, it's serious," McMoose said.
"Susie...I...what...how...tell her...you... a vampire?"

He can go a bit over the top. But that is something I can use.

"Let's have lunch," I said, "we can discuss my injury and how you will tell Susie over that lovely fish. Countess, where do you keep the plates?"

"Jack," McMoose said. "He bit you."

And so, once again, the great sleuth shows off his brilliant detective skills. I wonder if he had to sit an exam to be so stupid.

The fish smelled ready and so was my belly. Well, I think it was. It started making funny noises, my belly not the fish. The only noise the fish made was "eat me."

My belly rumbled again. I had a terrible taste in my mouth. I think I had gone for too long without food. Suddenly the room began to swirl around me.

My head felt light. McMoose was looking at me. His mouth was hanging open. An ugly mouse should never leave his mouth open, it doesn't help.

That was when I noticed the vampire hamsters looking at me as well.

"What?" I asked them. "I didn't do anything."

"I...am...so...sorry...Jack..." McMoose said.

"Sorry about what?"

"But you will be fine Jack...well...I am sure you will be fine."

Now he was worrying me.

"What do you mean?"

My hunger packed its bags and left me. A new pain took hunger's place.

"I just don't know how I will tell Susie she has a ...vampire cat," McMoose said.

"A what?" I shouted at him.

All of a sudden, I was craving...blood.

Chapter 10

I started shaking. "McMoose...blood...I...need..."

"Oh stop overacting," Countess Von Nibbles cut-in. "We don't drink blood, that's just a myth."

"I'm not overacting," I shouted at her.

"Anyway, it's only a small vampire bite," she said, "you won't change unless you feed."

"Feed?"

"Avoid food and you will be fine," she answered.

"But I'm starving," I cried. "I can't avoid food...I haven't eaten in days."

"Hours," McMoose said, "you ate on the train last night."

"Crumbs," I shouted. "Crumbs."

"It isn't that bad," Frank said. "Being a vampire is cool, as long as you can live without a reflection and don't mind going to vampire school at night."

My head was spinning. A life without my reflection was no life for a cat as cute as me. Without seeing my beauty in a mirror before bedtime, I had nothing to dream about.

My whole world was crumbling around me. My life was worse than over.

"We learn how to read at school," Frank's sister said. "My name's Ann and I love to read and you will like vampire school. We've never had a cat in vampire school, although, we did have a-"

"Are you...batty? I don't care-"

"Silly cat. I'm not a bat, I'm a vampire, we don't change into a bat, that's another silly myth," she said smiling.

"Now, now, McVamps," McMoose said, with his paws on his hips, "there's no need to panic. As the Countess said, a few days without food, you will be back to normal. Whatever normal is?"

"Panic? I have a right to panic. I'm going to starve away into nothing or worse. I'll turn into a vampire and never see my reflection ever again. I can't take this."

"A few days without food won't kill you," McMoose said cheerfully. "Why even a human can go thirty days without food."

"That long?" Ann asked him.

He scratched his chin and answered, "Well yes, however, that isn't really a good idea."

"Why not?" she asked him.

"Well you see without food a person can get terribly sick and they go through immense pain and discomfort, but I'm sure a...brave...cat like Mc...Jack...can make it."

Pain and discomfort. I was already in pain and discomfort, as I hadn't eaten since...I can't remember.

"Well as far as I recall," Countess Von Nibbles began, "you only need to stay off food for...Oh dear me...I can't recall exactly. Was it five or seven days?"

"How should I know?" I shouted.

"Temper, temper," McMoose said.

"Of course, I have a temper, what do you expect?"

"Seven," Ann said.

"Seven what?" I snapped at her. "Hours? Days? Weeks? What? Which?"

"Oh wait," she answered, "maybe it was five."

"Make it eight and you are guaranteed to be okay," Frank offered.

"Yes Jack, eight days without food," McMoose said smiling. "That's nothing for a...brave cat like you."

He laughed. I didn't find any of this funny.

"Hey, what's that noise?" Frank asked.

"My hungry belly, grumbling" I cried at them. "I need food!"

Everyone looked at me. At least someone was able to see me. I was going to have to spend the rest of my life relying on other people to describe how I looked.

I suppose being a vampire wouldn't be so bad after all. I could charge people to describe my cuteness. I am so cute people will pay to see me.

However, I would still miss my own reflection and that would only bring loneliness to me and countless mirrors. I wanted to cry, but then I noticed McMoose twitching his sleuthing ears.

"No, the sound is not his belly, I deduce it sounded like...wood hitting metal," he...deduced.

I have no idea what the word "deduce" meant. Nor did I care.

My problems needed solving and I had an even bigger problem in front of me than turning into a vampire. I was hungry and the steaming fish on the cooker was calling me.

It was a horrible temptation. I wanted that fish. I inched myself closer to the steaming pot while the vampire hamsters and the useless mouse tried to figure what the noise was, that they think they heard.

I looked around the room to make sure the coast was clear. All I saw was a room full of books on the collapsing shelves and piled up in neat stacks in the corners of the room next to worn chairs. I turned my attention back to the kitchen.

The kitchen table was set for lunch. I was so hungry.

The temptation was too much. I had to eat. I inched even closer to the pot.

"Cat, you made it," a voice shouted from the kitchen door.

I stopped dead in my tracks and looked at the happy smiling face of Count Von Nibbles. One second later and I would have had the lid off the pot. I hate these hamsters.

"My husband," Countess Von Nibbles shouted. "Look, kids, your daddy is home."

Frank and Ann shouted, even McMoose shouted, "Daddy."

He's such an idiot. I was getting cranky from hunger. I would have said crankier, but I was at the level of crankiness that can't go any higher.

"Why does everyone have to shout?" I shouted.

Countess Von Nibbles prodded her husband with her paw. "You are...real," she shouted.

"Why yes, what did you think, I was a ghost?" he laughed.

"He said you were," Countess Von Nibbles said looking at me.

"I only pretended to be a ghost to scare off the sailors on the train and stop them from getting the treasure," he said, hugging his wife.

"Sailors on a train?" Ann asked joining the embrace.

"Yes, it is a long story, he said, "let me start at the start, always good to start at the start, but first cat...I owe you a debt for taking care of my family like I asked of you."

McMoose took his bowler hat off. "Allow me to introduce myself, I am McMoose...Charles McMoose the sleuth, and the cat, his name is...Jack McSomething."

"McCuddles," I screamed, "my name is Jack McCuddles. Can't you get anything right?"

"Daddy I bit him by accident," Frank said.

"Indeed, but he will be fine," McMoose said to Count Von Nibbles while patting Frank on the shoulder. "The cat is disease free so young Frank will be fine."

"I am disease free!" I shouted at him. "I am...it was that little furry rodent that-"

"See everything will be okay," McMoose said to Count Von Nibbles. "Even the cat agrees he is disease free."

"Well I promised him pancakes for taking care of my family," Count Von Nibbles declared. "I'm not one to forget to pay a debt of gratitude."

Pancakes.

"So allow me to make everyone my world famous pancakes," Count Von Nibbles said.

Pancakes.

The kids cheered. McMoose smiled directly at me.

I knew why he was smiling even before he shook his head and twirled his paw around his belly.

"Pancakes sound wonderful," McMoose said, looking directly at me. He shook his head again. "Sadly Jack you will have to sit and watch us eat."

I looked away from him. I hated him. I wanted to go home and curl up next to Susie. I missed her and I knew she would look after me. Vampire infection or not, she would find some way to cure me, so I could eat.

I noticed Countess Von Nibbles' eyes looking sadly at her husband's paw and wooden leg.

"These," her husband said, lifting his left paw and his wooden leg. "Only a disguise, but I might keep the hook, really good for chopping onions."

McMoose stuck his bowler hat back on his head and looked at me. His face frowned and then softened. He quickly turned away from looking at me.

"I am sorry," McMoose said facing our hosts, "but we have no time to eat."

He looked at me and shrugged his shoulders. I think he was making excuses so I wouldn't have to watch everyone eat. Sometimes...and I mean sometimes as in rarely...but sometimes...he can be...kind.

"What? Why?" Ann asked him.

"Well you see there's still a mystery to solve," he answered. "I do believe I may have already solved the case, but I have need of your immediate help."

"What can we do?" Count Von Nibbles said, putting on his apron.

"I believe there is treasure, buried somewhere under the hotel and that the key to accessing the treasure is via the trapdoor at the bottom of your stairs."

"I already told Jack all of that when I met him on the train," Count Von Nibbles said looking at me.

Oops, I really should learn to listen.

"Indeed, you did," I piped up. "And I knew that the master sleuth that is McMoose...Charles McMoose would...de...umm...deduct the same conclusion."

Ann corrected me. "Deduce, like infer or to arrive at the conclusion."

"Yes, sorry the hunger is making my words not work right," I lied.

"Well if you had not deprived me of that information we could have been on the bus home by now," McMoose said, shaking his head at me.

"Deep fried you?"

"Deprived," Ann corrected me, again. "As in - you withheld information."

This was worse than school. I can't eat and now I am learning new words.

"I know what it means," I protested and lied. I didn't know what it meant, but they didn't need to know that. "That's what I said; I didn't want to...deep...prevent McMoose from solving the crime all by himself, after all...I'm only the "dishwasher" here."

"I see you two have much to talk about," Countess Von Nibbles said glaring at McMoose and then at me. "But my husband is home now; it has been a long week without him..."

"My dear, before I put on my furry slippers, we need to stop the descendant of the pirate Captain Green Beard," Count Von Nibbles said. "I lost him at the shipping port a few miles from here. I know he's on his way here. We need to act now."

"How did he discover the treasure?" McMoose asked them.

Countess Von Nibbles answered, "Pirate Captain Green Beard's great, great, great, great - grandson discovered the existence of a map to the buried treasure when they dug out the trees on the lawn of the hotel. It was tragic, those trees had existed there for centuries and then they got sick and so-"

"So," Frank said, putting the story back on track, "Captain Green Beard started scaring people off the train or dropping them off at the wrong station, that way the hotel would go broke and he could gain access to the hotel's cellar and dig for the treasure."

"First, I pretended to be a ghost on his ship," Count Von Nibbles said, "I scared off his crew from his pirate ship that was due to anchor off our lighthouse and then I scared off his remaining crew on the train."

"Do you have proof that this Captain Green Beard is behind all of this?" McMoose asked him.

"Proof?" Count Von Nibbles asked him.

"Yes, proof?"

"Well, not really."

McMoose stared at the ceiling. "Not good," he muttered.

I didn't see anything wrong with the ceiling that a lick of paint wouldn't fix.

"Does know about the trapdoor located here?" McMoose inquired.

"Gosh no, only we vampire hamsters know about that," Ann said.

McMoose shook his confused head slowly.

"We?" he asked them.

"Yes, we," Count Von Nibbles said. "As I explained to McCuddles on the train-"

The fish was still steaming away in the pot and had formed a moist covering of condensation on the window. My hunger was so great that it made me move closer to the window.

I watched little dribbles of water roll down the window. I stuck out my tongue to catch one. But something was wrong.

My tongue was stuck between two of my teeth. It had never done that before.

McMoose stared at me. "McCuddles, what else did he explain to you on the train that you have forgotten to mention?"

I was tongue-tied.

Count Von Nibbles gave me an odd stare before he started speaking, "A hamster city exists under the lighthouse and is connected by a tunnel to the hotel. If Captain Green Beard goes into the hotel cellar and starts digging, he will undoubtedly destroy our city. The treasure he is looking for is located above the heads of every living vampire hamster down there. That is why he must be stopped."

"The fish must be ready," Frank said, moving beside me, "shall we continue this over food? There's enough for everyone."

I didn't want to change into a vampire, so for the first time in my life, I was about to refuse food. But McMoose spoke up and saved me the embarrassment of saying no to food.

"No," he said sternly. "I cannot let Jack near food. I do not want to see the ass-"

He stopped and looked at me. We all waited for him to finish his sentence. I wanted to defend myself and tell him I am a cat, the cutest cat in the world and not a donkey or an ass. But my tongue was still trapped between my teeth.

McMoose heaved a deep breath and announced, "I have great need of the ass...my assistant sleuth. We have a city to protect, a hotel to save and a pirate to stop."

"Oh he's not a real pirate," Count Von Nibbles said, "Captain Green Beard runs a pirate ship amusement ride."

"Well whatever he is, we must stop him," McMoose said. "Come on McCuddles...the games-apaw."

"Afoot," Ann corrected him. "The games afoot."

Count Von Nibbles raised his left leg and said, "It will be jolly fun to play football again."

"Dad," Frank said, wiping some of the condensation off the window with his paw, "I thought you said you scared off Captain Green Beard's pirate ship?"

"I did," he replied.

"Then who owns that big ship out there with the Jolly Roger flag?"

We all crowded around the window.

"No," I screamed, "no, it can't be."

"We can still save the day," McMoose said.

"Not the ship you idiot, me, look...I can't see...me."

Chapter 11

"You're such a silly cat," Ann said, wiping the window around where my reflection should have been.

The more she wiped the window with her paw the clearer my reflection greeted me. I looked amazing in the window's reflection. I smiled at my reflection and it smiled back. Well, of course, it smiled back at me, anything that can catch my reflection falls in love with me.

Everyone was "oohing" and "awning" really loudly around me. At first, I thought it was because of my reflection, so I looked at them and I was about to say thank you. Then I noticed their eyes were on the ship and not on me. To say that saddened me is an understatement, such selfishness should be against the law.

The ship was a huge wooden monster with square-rigged sails and oars sticking out of the sides. A flag waved from the topmost mast. It had a skull with two crossing swords under the skull.

"It's his ship," Count Von Nibbles said. "But how did he get a crew to sail here? I was sure I scared them all off."

"Daddy," Frank said, "I count ten cannons on this side."

"If my calculations are correct," Ann said, "from this distance, he will have no problem destroying our home or the hotel."

"I think your home is safe, but I fear for the hotel," McMoose said.

"Come on you two, I may need your help," Ann said.

"With what?" I said to my reflection.

I am so cute. Even when I am starving and turning into a vampire. I still look cute.

I felt a paw pull my left ear. But I saw nothing move in the reflective surface of the window.

"I'll show you," Ann said, pulling me away from the window. "We need to get to the city and launch the submarine."

"Submarine?" I asked her.

"How else can vampire hamster travel during daylight?" Frank said laughing. "We can't exactly fly an airplane in the sunlight."

"And besides," Countess Von Nibbles added, "where would we land a plane on this island?"

"We have no time to waste," Ann said. "McMoose, get back over the mainland and warn Lord McBedbugs that his hotel is in danger."

"Will do," McMoose agreed.

"I'll relay coordinates from here via radio," Count Von Nibbles said to Ann. "Tell Captain Von Leaks...we must sink that ship...at all costs."

"Aye, aye," Ann cheered running for the door to the stairs.

Ann was still gripping my ear so I had no choice but to follow her. She bounced down the stairs with speed and with my ear in her paw. My own paws barely touched the steps. By the time we made it to the bottom of the lighthouse, I was a wreck.

Ann didn't seem to notice. She pulled open the trapdoor and jumped down into the darkness shouting, "Come on McCuddles."

I looked into the blackness left over from the open trapdoor. I turned and looked at the door with a big metal, unbreakable padlock attached to it. The door led outside to the island.

At no point did I think about running outside and taking the rowing boat to the mainland, nor did I even think about finding a warm spot on the island to hide in.

I did give the padlock a quick security test, well just in case the pirates tried to break-in. My paws slipped when I pulled down on the padlock and I fell backward. Trapdoors should never be left open.

I went crashing through the hole left in the ground by the open trapdoor. I landed in a small wooden box. My bum hurt.

I looked up and saw that Ann had her paws above her head on some rope. She started pushing and pulling on the rope. The wooden box began to move. I felt metal wheels rumble slowly over metal tracks.

"Hold tight," she ordered.

Her paws let go of the rope and the box started to move slowly downwards. I think she was being a bit dramatic about telling me to hold tight. The box moved slowly down the tracks and into the darkness. Chug, chug, we went past a few dangling light bulbs hanging from the rock ceiling.

Then suddenly the box moved on a quick downwards trajectory. Big chunks of rock faced me on both sides. I threw my paws up to my face and protected my cuteness from the sharp edged rocks. The noise of my screams was deafening me, but it was better than the loud chugging of speeding wheels on metal.

The box came to a sudden halt, not soon enough for my belly. I was seasick and shaken. I fell forwards. Then it chugged, slowly again.

"This is my city," Ann said as we chugged along the tracks.

I opened my paws and then my eyes and looked around. Bright lights blinded me.

My eyes stung and adjusted to the glare. I saw lights attached to the small buildings and many multi-colored lights of odd shapes hanging from the cave ceiling.

The streets around the buildings were jammed with hamsters. I had never seen so many in my life. It must have been rush hour, but I honestly had no idea what would make a hamster rush anywhere.

"That's my school over there," Ann said, pointing at a big building.

The school was a red brick building with three floors. It looked scary, but all schools look like that. Places you would never walk into unless forced to do so by parents.

Beside it was a tall gray building with a big sign saying in bright red letters: "Our History."

"And that's the museum," she smiled proudly. "And over there is the cod liver oil store..."

"The what?"

"Oh you don't know, we don't drink blood, we eat cod liver oil tablets."

I almost wanted to be sick. The aftertaste of those tablets requires hours of strong, minty fresh toothpaste to remove or Root Beer. However, Root Beer has lots of sugar so of course, Susie just gave me toothpaste when she makes me take cod liver oil tablets.

"I wish I had time to show you around, but we must head for the launch pad," Ann said sadly.

"Lunch-pad, but I can't eat," I objected.

"No silly, the submarine launch pad, it's just around this corner."

Our box came to a stop. Ann jumped out and I followed. She ran down around the corner. We were greeted by the biggest amount of shiny metal I had ever seen.

It was a submarine, but that is not important. I looked beautiful reflected off the metal of the submarine.

I wasn't given time to admire this great achievement.

"Magnificent to look at," Ann said. "But we don't have time to sit around and admire..."

Well, I wasn't expecting her to say magnificent. I usually get cute, adorable or just speechlessness when my cuteness is on display.

Ann grabbed my ear just as I discovered that my green eyes dazzled wondrously off the shiny submarine surface. She dragged me up a long wooden ladder by my ear to an open hatch on top of the submarine.

She jumped down and forgot to release my ear. I landed inside the submarine with a small patch of fur missing off my ear.

I looked up and saw a black haired hamster dressed in a shiny white shirt and skirt smiling down at me.

"Permission to come aboard, Captain?" Ann asked her.

"Permission granted, the torpedoes are armed and awaiting your attention," she said with a commanding voice. "And who may I ask is this?"

"That's McCuddles, we may need him for the engines if the torpedoes don't do the job," Ann replied.

"Very well, follow me, McCuddles. I am Captain Von Leaks."

"A pleasure," I said. "But I don't know how I can be of help?"

"See you later McCuddles," Ann said.

She ran down the dark and cramped corridor to the front of the submarine. The submarine was not designed for a cat my size. I discovered this every time my head hit the ceiling.

"Perhaps," I began, "perhaps I should go ashore as this boat isn't..."

"This is a submarine, not a boat," Captain Von Leaks said.

What is it about these hamsters and their need to educate me?

"Sorry, as I was saying, I am far too big for this boa-...submarine and perhaps I should go ashore?"

"Permission denied," she replied. "There is only one rule on my

66

submarine when I give an order you reply..." Captain Von Leaks paused, over the loud sound of the hatch above my head locking.

She waited as a few hamsters dressed in gray uniforms saluted and scurried past us.

I got bored waiting.

"Yes?" I asked her. "What is the reply?"

"Captain," she replied. "Yes, Captain."

These hamsters are a fussy bunch. Anyone else would be happy with a yes, but oh no, it has to be "yes Captain."

"Sorry, yes...Captain."

"Good, now that you know the rule, follow me."

I must have missed something. I need to listen better, but in my defense, she didn't' actually say the rule. She didn't strike me as the type of hamster to explain herself, twice, let alone once. So instead of asking again, I followed her silently down a cramped corridor.

"This is the command center and the sonar room," she said to me. "Find something to hold on to."

I looked at her puzzled. The room was even more cramped than the corridor. Two hamsters sat at their steering wheels. Another sat in the corner with headphones attached to his ears.

"Ready?" the captain asked the room and no one in particular that I could see.

"Yes, Captain," one of the hamsters at the steering wheel, replied.

"Prepare to depart," she said.

"Yes, Captain," the other hamster at the steering wheel, replied.

I heard a swooshing noise fill the room. Then a beep-beep sound. The floor beneath my paws felt like it was moving. My belly moved upwards in my chest. I felt like I was being pushed upwards.

"Captain, the submarine is secure, airlocks closed, we have a green light," the hamster with the headphones said.

"Launch!" she bellowed.

Lunch already?

But I wasn't allowed to eat. I was about to protest when the floor trembled worse than my empty belly.

The submarine shifted at a weird angle. I started to slip on the floor towards the back of the command center.

"Hold fast, McCuddles," Captain Von Leaks ordered.

"What's a fast?" I shouted.

I didn't like the look I got back.

Anyway, it was too late to hold onto anything. The submarine shifted upwards at ninety degrees. Okay, I say ninety degrees. It shot upwards. It might have been eighty degrees. What do I know? All I know is that I flew downwards to the bottom of the compartment and banged my head.

The submarine kept moving upwards. My ears popped, my belly...well, it went a bit gassy. The compartment filled up with a horrid smell.

I closed my nose and eyes and shouted, "It wasn't me."

Chapter 12

"Captain, we are on course for the pirate ship," the hamster with the headphones said.

"Sonar, ping the ship and get a fix, transfer the data to Ann," the captain ordered him. She picked up a phone hanging from the ceiling and shouted, "Ann ready torpedoes tubes one and four."

I heard a squawking noise as I made my way to the middle of the command center. I think it was Ann answering the captain and not the fear in my empty belly.

"Ship ahead, Captain," the sonar hamster said.

"Rise to periscope depth," the captain ordered.

"Rising," a voice said.

"Up periscope," the captain ordered.

The periscope slowly descended from the ceiling. The captain put her eyes to it and took in a deep breath.

Without taking her eyes from the viewfinder on the periscope she ordered, "Left one degree."

I watched the hamster on the left move his steering wheel and then say, "Left one degree, Captain."

"Sonar?" she called out.

"Details sent to Ann."

The captain picked up the dangling phone, "Fire torpedoes one and four."

I heard the squawk sound and seconds later, I felt the greatest release of air - well the greatest since the last time I ate four tins of beans in one sitting - shake the submarine.

The captain peered into the periscope.

We waited. The engine rumbled. Everyone went silent.

Then we all heard a "boing" noise fill the room.

"Nothing," the captain cried into the periscope.

The dangling phone rang loudly from the ceiling.

I heard the squawking noises. The captain looked directly at me.

"Captain, we are being pinged," the sonar hamster shouted.

"All silent," the captain announced into the phone.

The submarine went deadly silent. I heard every rumble of my belly over the silence. The submarine shuddered slightly and then the room filled up with a terrible high-pitched pinging sound.

"They've located us," the sonar hamster shouted. "Firing cannons, one...two...three."

"Prepare for impact," the captain shouted into the phone.

I heard a loud rumble noise pass above the submarine.

The sonar hamster shouted, "Miss."

"I think she prefers to be called Captain," I shouted back at him.

I try my best to be helpful. I have no idea why the captain looked at me and then shook her head.

But he didn't shout "Miss" for the second and third cannon ball. I was right and I was about to say so when I heard something smash against the exterior of the submarine.

Suddenly a gush of water hit me in the face.

From out of nowhere, two hamsters ran into the command center and started sticking newspapers and sawdust into the hole where the water was escaping and attacking me.

"Captain, it won't hold for long," one of the hamsters shouted.

"Take the cat to the engine room, we have no choice, but to go with Ann's plan," the captain ordered her hamsters.

"What plan?" I shouted as they ushered me from the command center.

I received no answer from her.

They pushed and prodded me down a dark corridor. Then they shoved me into a room with two huge hamster wheels. Four hamsters stood on one of the wheels looking at me.

A hamster covered in sawdust greeted me, but not in a friendly manner, "Cat, get on the wheel, we are going to ram them and need all the power we can get."

"Why?"

"To force that ship onto the rocks and ground them on the beach."

"Not that why. Why do you need me on the wheel?"

"We need all the power we can get, and I can't get enough power for the captain out of my hamsters."

I was in a state of shock. They wanted me, the cutest cat in the world to run around on a hamster wheel. I was about to protest. The idea was deplorable and humiliating. How dare they expect me to run around on a hamster wheel?

The captain's voice filled up the engine room before I could utter a word of objection.

"Get that cat running now," her voice commanded, "we need all the power we can get."

"Hurry," the engineer shouted, "onto the wheel and run for your life."

He didn't give me much of an option. He pulled me into the hamster wheel.

The floor of the wheel was littered with sawdust. I don't know why hamsters have sawdust on the floor of their cages or wheels for that matter.

The engineer prodded me and I ran for my life. I wasn't going anywhere. The wheel spun over my head. Sawdust rained down on my head. I was panting and breathing in sawdust. It took all my power not to sneeze. I didn't have the energy to sneeze. These wheels take a lot out of you.

"Faster," the engineer shouted at me.

I glanced to my right and saw the other four hamsters running on their wheel. I hoped I didn't look at silly as they did and that nobody had a camera with them.

The engineer picked up a phone from the ceiling and shouted, "Captain we are giving you all we have got."

He dropped the phone from his paw and shouted at us:

"Prepare for impact."

I ran and ran as the submarine crashed into the pirate ship.

I nearly fell off the wheel, but somehow the engineer was able to stop me and keep me on the spinning wheel. I felt sick and dizzy and this odd wet and stingy substance was dripping into my eyes.

It was sweat!

My sweat and it was flowing towards my mouth. My heart was

beating so fast it was filling my ears with cries to stop running.

"Here we go again," the engineer shouted, "faster and hold tight."

The submarine hit the pirate ship again. I slipped but somehow found my footing and kept running. Don't ask me how. I was in shock from running so much and from sweating so much I really had no idea what was going on.

The captain's voice shouted over the submarine's intercom:

"We have done it, the pirate ship is aground."

A cheer echoed down every corridor of the submarine. Then I heard a cracking noise from somewhere around me.

The walls to the side exploded with a rush of water flooding into the compartment.

"We are flooding," the engineer screamed.

As if, he needed to tell us that.

He shouted again, "Everyone out and to the escape pods."

At least that was useful.

My wobbly legs found some strength and I jumped from my wheel and followed the exhausted hamsters out of the flooding compartment. We left the compartment and entered the next one. The water in the second compartment was up to my neck and around my legs. The poor hamsters struggled to stay afloat.

"All aboard the cat," the engineer ordered his hamsters.

Before I was able to voice my concern, the hamsters had clambered onto my back.

"Head straight," the engineer, ordered me.

I ran through the submarine as more and more hamsters climbed aboard my back. By the time, we made it to the escape pods; I was ready to collapse from their weight.

I saw Ann standing beside some boxes next to the torpedo tubes. She looked concerned. She should be. Carry all these hamsters was bad for my back.

"Everyone into a pod," she ordered.

One by one, they jumped off me.

"The guidance system will take you back to the city," Ann shouted.

I watched the hamsters jump into the small boxes and be loaded into the torpedoes tubes by Ann. Ann kept loading and firing them from the torpedo tubes until the room was empty except for her and me.

"Good job," a drenched Captain Von Leaks said, from the doorway.

"Captain, one and four tubes are set for automatic firing," Ann said to the captain. "But what about McCuddles?"

"Oh dear, we don't have an escape pod for him," the captain said, shaking her head at me. "Well all you have to do," she said, tapping the torpedo tube, "is climb into this tube and when it fills with water you will rush up and into the sea. The land isn't far from where we are now, so you should be okay."

"Should be?" I questioned her logic.

"Have you forgotten the rules of my submarine?" she asked me sternly.

Forgotten them? I hadn't even a clue what they were.

"Have you forgotten I'm a cat and not a duck?"

"Jack," Ann said pushing me towards the tube, "the rules of the submarine."

"What about them?"

"Yes, Captain," Ann saluted.

The poor hamster was hearing voices. "She didn't say anything to you."

"That's the rule, silly, when your captain gives an order, you say, yes, Captain."

"The tube McCuddles, into the tube, that's an order," Captain Von Leaks...ordered me.

"But?"

"No buts, into the tube now," Captain Von Leaks said, "that's an order and failure to follow an order results in a court-martial."

I wonder if they serve pancakes and real maple syrup in Hamster Navy Prison.

"Please Jack, you must get in the tube," Ann pleaded.

It seems I had no say in the matter. Ann grabbed my left ear and lifted me off the floor. For something so small, she is very strong.

I felt a sharp kick on my bum. Suddenly I found myself crammed inside the torpedo tube.

I screamed. As usual, no one was listening to me.

I don't ask for much from life.

All I need is a nice warm fire to snuggle beside, a mirror close at paw for when I wish to admire myself, lots of attention when I demand it and mountains of food, within easy reach of my paws.

Is that too much to ask for?

Chapter 13

The tube was cramped, wet and dark. I heard the door clink shut behind my tail as a small door opened above my head. Water came gushing in and surrounded me. I held what little air I had in my lungs and closed my eyes.

From somewhere close to my backside, a great rush of air pushed me upwards and I went spinning out of the tube and into the water surrounding the submarine.

Well, I think I did. I had my eyes closed. But only to protect them from the seawater, not from fear.

I was traveling at such a great velocity I hit the surface in seconds. My head was a bit dizzy but I was able to open my eyes.

I looked up and saw the sun above my head and when I looked back down again I got a fright. I saw sea, miles and miles of sea, with no land in sight.

This was it. I knew it. I wanted to cry. I was doomed and destined to float towards the empty horizon and never see myself in a mirror again or food or land.

It was hopeless. I was lost, lost at sea.

The sun was beating down on my head. I was thirsty and hungry. I knew the stages of my doom from reading a book once about shipwrecked pirates, miles from land.

It was horrible to read. The words were big and the book was old, yellow and smelly. It even had little bugs on the pages. I didn't read the whole book. I felt dirty. However, from what I read, I knew what was going to happen to me.

My need for water would eventually force me to drink from the sea. The salt in the seawater will bring on a terrible sickness, followed by madness. When I am not sick, a hunger will take over me. I will be forced to chop off my paw and nibble on it.

My paw. I love my paw. I use it to scratch my ears. The horror I must endure, with only the hope of a rescue to keep me company.

I was at the mercy of the sea. All hope was gone.

My mind started to fill up with images of a warm cozy fireplace. My reflection in a mirror and lovely pancakes covered in real maple syrup beside me. It was the madness taking a hold of me and so soon. I had expected a few more minutes before the madness came.

Soon, I knew, the hallucinations from the sun beating down on my head will start. What would I see?

"McCuddles...come here."

Voices I was hearing voices. The sun was playing tricks with my mind. The hallucinations had started.

The worst part was that the hallucination sounded like McMoose.

"Oh no, he's not..."

"Oh yes, he is..."

The voices sounded like a pantomime.

"Look behind you!" the voices sang.

I refused to listen to the voices in my head.

"I say, look behind you."

Never. I kept my eyes ahead of me. If this was my doom, I wasn't going to answer the voices. I was going to be brave.

"We have food."

I turned away from the empty horizon and looked behind me.

McMoose was standing on the beach. He was a mirage. The sun was playing tricks with my eyes. Standing beside him was Count Von Nibbles. He was wearing a dark cloak covering most of his furry face.

"I told you he was alive," McMoose said, walking into the sea. "Come on McCuddles we don't have time for you to laze around in the water and sunbathe."

The cruelest of mirages.

"Leave me be," I cried, "I don't deserve this, let me face my doom bravely and without you in my mirage."

"What did he say?" Count Von Nibbles asked.

McMoose grabbed my tail and started to pull me to the beach.

"Snap out of it McCuddles or we will miss lunch," he said.

"Lunch? You mean you are real?" I said feeling the sand under my legs.

"Yes, and I'm starving after chasing all those pirates off that ship."

I looked over his shoulder and saw the pirate ship on the beach. A big hole was in the side where the submarine had nudged it onto the beach.

"I'm alive," I shouted. "I'm alive...what's for lunch?"

The hooded figure of Count Von Nibbles approached me and said, "Well when Ann gets back, we will be having fish, potatoes, and some peas and...oh wait, Frank's bitten you..."

"I almost forgot, sorry no lunch for you McCuddles," McMoose said, "and thanks, Count Von Nibbles for all your help, now you had better get inside before the sun gets to you."

"Why yes, I can smell the smoke from my cloak already, so glad I could help," Count Von Nibbles smiled. "Till later then."

"Yes," McMoose said. "And thank you again."

Count Von Nibbles waved as McMoose and I set off towards the hotel.

"Wonderful chap," McMoose said as I trailed behind him. "One look at his fangs and those pirates ran for the hills. I would never have succeeded without him. I wish I had a partner like him on all my cases."

"What about me?" I tiredly asked him.

"You," he said stopping and turning to look at me. "What did you do other than sink a submarine?"

"I did not," I cried.

"All we saw was the escape pods heading towards the lighthouse after a torpedo hit the pirate ship."

"But."

"Let me guess you got in the way and your bum hit the submarine's steering wheel and forced it to crash."

"No, I did not."

"Well I am soaked from having to drag your lazy body from the sea, so if it's okay with you, I will change my clothes and get some lunch.

"That is not..."

"I don't really care what you have to say. We have one problem sorted and one to solve, so as long as I don't get a bill for a new submarine, we will let the matter lie."

"But, that's not what happened."

He continued walking ahead of me towards the hotel. I was tired, hungry and had bits of sand and seaweed stuck to my fur. I needed to bathe and I needed sleep.

I wished I had the energy to set him straight, but I don't think he really cared about anything I said, or cared about me.

I was lonely. I needed Susie. She'd listen to me and tell me I am cute and wonderful.

We arrived at the hotel. Lord McBedbugs was on the hotel steps to greet us. He looked happy.

"I see you had much of a to-do this morning," he remarked to us pointing in the direction of the shipwreck.

"Yes, but I have one problem solved," McMoose said.

"Yes, it will be jolly fun for all the kiddies to play on my new pirate ship," Lord McBedbugs said, rubbing his hands, "more money for me."

"Wait," I said, "that ship belongs to Captain Green Beard."

"I claimed the salvage," Lord McBedbugs smiled. "And once you prove he is guilty of his crimes he will be in jail and have no need of anything."

Something was off and it wasn't the smell from the kitchen. I had a sudden feeling Lord McBedbugs was not on the level.

I had a problem. I had no idea why I felt something was off about Lord McBedbugs and I knew McMoose wasn't going to listen to a word I had to say.

"What's for lunch?" McMoose asked him.

"Chicken, it will be served in ten minutes, although I do suggest you get out of those wet clothes before dining in my restaurant."

"Will do," McMoose said, "until lunch."

"Till lunch," Lord McBedbugs said as he departed for the kitchen.

All this talk of lunch was clouding my mind. Something was off, it was on the tip of my tongue, between my whiskers and my...

"Fangs!" I screamed.

"What?" McMoose asked me.

I opened my mouth and showed him.

"Yuck, close your mouth, your breath smells."

"Fangs," I said pointing with my paw. "I have fangs."

"Yes, so?"

"So, so...so? I haven't eaten and I'm growing fangs."

"Why yes, of course, you missed it when you took your little trip in the submarine that you sunk. Countess Von Nibbles did remark that you will temporarily change into a vampire, but as long as you don't eat for thirteen days you will be fine."

"Thirteen days? Since when?"

"Since when? From when you were bitten."

"No," I cried, "when did it become thirteen days without food? It was only supposed to be eight."

"Well no one is really certain, but Countess Von Nibbles thinks it might be thirteen. But not to worry this change is only temporary."

"I can do a spell and make it go away," I said.

"If you want Susie to ever have a chance of getting her Witch License back then you won't break the law."

"But what if I was trapped in a train carriage and had to use magic to open the door?"

McMoose gave me a look that gave me goose bumps.

"Have you used your magic?" he asked.

"No," I lied. "Why do you ask such a thing?"

He shook his head and let out a grumble.

I think it was a grumble, although there was a strange smell. But that could have been me. Hunger was giving me a windy belly.

"If you don't use your magic and I get this case solved, I might be able to get her license back," McMoose said.

"How?"

"I do believe...it will be an interesting...lunch. Come on McCuddles, we need to change for...lunch."

I hate him. Any sane person would answer my question. But not him.

He has to wander off with a mysterious air around him. Well, the mysterious air wasn't all that mysterious. Not eating was playing havoc with my belly. Between the smell of dirty seawater and smells from my backside, I stank.

My fangs had grown a bit bigger. I did think that biting McMoose was a bad idea. Only because I am not allowed to eat anything and I don't know my way home.

As for the great mystery involving the vampire hamsters, Captain Green Beard, and Lord McBedbugs. I hadn't a clue what was going on.

I suspect, McMoose was only pretending to know what was going on.

Chapter 14

McMoose changed into another of his blue suits while I took a nap on the bed after some grooming. My fangs made washing a bit of a chore. I waited until I was clean before glancing at my timeless cuteness in the mirror. At least I still had my reflection.

McMoose didn't provide me with any more clues as to how he was going to get Susie's license back. He only spoke when he ordered me to follow him to the dining room.

I did as ordered. The thoughts of seeing food and not being allowed to eat any was distressing me.

We entered the dining room and McMoose climbed up onto the table next to the window. I think he was afraid that if he sits on a chair, someone would squash him by accident. It is a theory I yearn to test.

I took a seat next to the window. I looked pale in the glass.

One other guest was sitting across the room from us. I was so consumed with hunger and the strange smell coming from the kitchen that I didn't pass many remarks to him.

However, he made his presence known to us.

"Aye laddie, I see ye made it," he said approaching our table.

I recognized the pirate outfit immediately.

"The train conductor," I gasped, jumping from my seat and onto the floor.

I had my teeth bared. Ready to bite and defend myself.

"Captain Green Beard I presume," McMoose said, extending his paw.

"May I?" Captain Green Beard said, indicating my empty seat.

"By all means," McMoose replied.

Captain Green Beard sat on the seat and smiled. He smelled funny, a cross between seaweed and chicken.

"So laddie, ye sink me ship, well what do ye have to say for yourself?" he asked me.

"You fired on us first," I said.

"Only after ye fired on me, first."

"You were attacking the lighthouse," I said. "And you had the Jolly Roger flying on your ship."

"I was protecting them, laddie, protecting them vampire hamsters."

"I thoughts as much," McMoose said.

Captain Green Beard gave McMoose a cold hard stare with his one good eye. "Then why did ye chase off me scurvy crew when me ship did run aground?"

"Sorry about that, but I had to be certain," McMoose answered.

"Certain of what?" I asked him.

"Look here is our host Lord McBedbugs," McMoose announced.

Lord McBedbugs walked leisurely over to our table. No wonder his hotel is empty. He should be rushing over to take our lunch order with some breadsticks in a basket to keep us happy with until our starters arrived.

I so wanted to eat.

"Lunch will be served presently," Lord McBedbugs said greeting us.

His greeting was short lived when he saw Captain Green Beard.

"You!" he shouted.

"Aye it's me alright and I have come to honor my family," Captain Green Beard said.

"He's the criminal," Lord McBedbugs shouted. "He's the one you are after, arrest him."

"Firstly," McMoose said, "I am a sleuth and no longer work for the Mice Police, so I have no power to arrest anyone and secondly, he hasn't actually committed any crimes."

I was getting confused. Hunger does that to a cat or maybe this convoluted mystery was getting to me. And yes I did have to look it up, convoluted means complicated but convoluted sounds more convoluting...so hungry. I was not making any sense, even to myself.

"I need to EAT!" I screamed.

No one cares about my needs.

"I demand you arrest him," Lord McBedbugs shouted.

"For what?" Captain Green Beard asked him.

I provided an answered for him, "Well you did try to scare us off the train and drop us off at the wrong station. And you did make me clean the floor and eat crumbs and..."

"Aye laddie, I had heard a great sleuth was on the train and was hired to stop me from honoring my family. I apologize for being cruel, but I had mistaken ye for the great sleuth. But the chickens would have done ye no harm when I unlocked your door and let ye wander into their compartment."

"So it wasn't my magic spell that opened the door," I exclaimed. "But why did you let them into my carriage to attack me?"

"I didn't," he replied. "You insulted them. Chickens are very strange, laddie."

"What spell?" McMoose demanded to know. "What door? What spell McLiar?"

"We really should deal with the issue the issue at hand," I said smiling at McMoose. "After all, Lord McBedbugs is paying you to solve a mystery for him."

"True I have a mystery to solve and now that I have all the suspects before me I will start," he said pacing around on the table.

"This man has tried to ruin my business," Lord McBedbugs shouted while pointing his right-hand finger at Captain Green Beard.

"Not I, sir," Captain Green Beard said, rising to his feet and stabbing his finger in Lord McBedbugs direction. "Not I sir, but you sir," he said firmly.

"Who sir?" Lord McBedbugs demanded with his pointy finger. "Not I sir, but you sir...you ruffian."

"Me sir, a ruffian?" Captain Green Beard shouted, with his finger wagging while he inched closer to Lord McBedbugs.

"Three bags full sir," shouted Countess Von Nibbles from the doorway.

She was waving three big brown bags in her paws. I was happy to see her. Otherwise, Green Beard and McBedbugs would have gone on forever pointing and wagging their fingers at each other.

"McCuddles you only need to starve for six days," Countess Von Nibbles announced, "but if you do eat by accident..."

"How can you accidently eat?" McMoose asked her.

"Accidents can happen," I said, "why there was this one time when I fell into a bowl of maple syrup and..."

"No, no," Countess Von Nibbles said, shaking her head, "you must not eat, but if you do eat then straight away you must eat one of these."

She raised the bag higher.

The smell wafted over in my direction. It was an awful smell. It reminded me of the smell from McMoose's socks and underwear on washday.

You should see the bathtub after him, yuck.

"Raw garlic," Countess Von Nibbles smiled.

"When you are quite done with your cooking lesson," an impatient Lord McBedbugs said, "we still have the matter of this ruffian and what you are going to do with him."

"Raw garlic, no...I can't...I will have to starve," I screamed.

I was being brave, but I think my scream was confusing to Lord McBedbugs. His finger stopped pointing and closed in his hand to form a fist.

McMoose gasped.

He saw the punch that Captain Green Beard didn't see coming.

Lord McBedbugs' fist landed on Green Beard's chin. The noise that the connecting fist made was crunchy enough to make my belly churn.

The captain staggered back across the room. He had no control over his feet or the direction he was going. He was heading for the table that McMoose was standing on.

I should have shouted a warning, but...tables are easy to fix.

Captain Green Beard hit the table with all his weight, and if I am being honest, he was carrying a bit more than he should. I blame too much sugar.

He hit the table and thankfully, the table took the full brunt of his weight without breaking. Sadly, he missed McMoose. The captain rolled off the table and fell onto the floor.

A shocked McMoose shouted at me, "Stop him."

"Who?" I asked him.

"You idiot," he screamed.

"Me? What did I do?"

"Not you...you idiot...him," McMoose pointed.

I followed his paw and saw the departing figure of Lord McBedbugs. He can move when he wants to, not like when I needed him to move and bring me breakfast.

"Why?" I asked McMoose. "Perhaps he has gone to get breadsticks."

"He's the one we are after. He's the one after the treasure."

"Then why doesn't he just dig it up?

"McIdiot what are you rambling on about?"

I am a smart cat. I wish, just once, he would acknowledge my greatness.

"The treasure is in his cellar," I said. "After all, the hotel belongs to him."

"McCuddles are you a complete idiot. Captain Green Beard isn't the baddie...Lord McBedbugs is, now run off and fetch him."

"I am not a dog and I will not play fetch."

"Aye laddie, we need to stop him," Captain Green Beard said, holding his chin. "Stop him before he destroys the vampire hamster city."

"Will someone please explain to me what's going on here?" Countess Von Nibbles asked.

Of course, all along, I had suspected that Lord McBedbugs was up to no good. But I wasn't able to pin down the reason why. Therefore, I said nothing.

I wanted McMoose to solve this mystery all by himself. Anyway, now it was too late to reveal my brilliance to the room and accuse Lord McBedbugs of...of...the mystery he had made. Therefore, I waved my paw in McMoose's direction and allowed him to explain everything. You see, I can be unselfish.

"Lord McBedbugs hired me," McMoose said, "but I knew something was odd." McMoose looked over at Captain Green Beard and continued, "You did an excellent job trying to stop us from arriving here."

"Thank you," Captain Green Beard said. "From a master sleuth like you, that is indeed a compliment. I believed Lord McBedbugs had hired you to stop me from my duty."

"I am even more confused now," Countess Von Nibbles

frowned.

"Indeed," McMoose said to her, "it was what you said Countess, about the trees that helped me make solve..."

"Of course," I shouted, "the treasure map."

"Yes, the treasure map, and you have seen the treasure, McCuddles."

"I have? Where? I mean yes...Of course, I have...the treasure...umm...shiny and made of...treasure."

"Indeed, and it shines above the vampire hamster city," McMoose said.

"And when I heard from a traveling vampire hamster that the map had been found," Captain Green Beard said, "I knew I needed to come back here and honor my family duty."

"I don't understand," Countess Von Nibbles said.

"Let me explain," Captain Green Beard said. "Well, you see my great, great, grandfather was a pirate and he established your city as a home for the vampire hamsters he found on his travels. He laid his vast wealth of treasure into the roof of the cave-"

"Why?" I asked him.

McMoose said, "Light, McCuddles, light."

I stared at him.

"It isn't dark."

"He's right," Countess Von Nibbles said.

"Of course, I am," I smiled at her.

She glanced at me and said, "The gems provide light, beautiful colorful displays over the city. Imagine always having Christmas trees lights lit up all year round. Cheers us up no end to see such a colorful display."

"Especially as the vampire hamsters cannot go out often in daylight," Captain Green Beard said.

"It truly was a wonderful gift," Countess Von Nibbles said. "But why did Lord McBedbugs hire you?"

"He figured I would stop Captain Green Beard," McMoose answered. "That would give him the time to steal all the treasure for himself."

McMoose looked sadly at Captain Green Beard. "I did suspect you, sorry." Then he pointed at me and said, "Well until he rammed your ship."

"Understandable now," Captain Green Beard said, "I believed you were in the employ of Lord McBedbugs and I had to do everything to defend the vampire hamsters."

All this patting each other on the back for being clever was boring me to tears.

I spoke to directly to McMoose, "This is far too complicated. Why didn't Lord McBedbugs just dig up the treasure? He has a map and the treasure is under his hotel."

"It isn't his," Count Von Nibbles said, "the hotel belongs to the vampire hamster city."

I was shocked. "What?"

"Correct, even Lord McBedbugs admitted that he paid rent for the hotel," McMoose said.

"When?" I demanded. "When did he say that?"

McMoose answered, "One must follow...every clue... listen to the smallest detail...no matter how small...no matter how-"

I had to stop him. Otherwise, he would have gone on for hours.

"When?" I cut-in. "Just say when that's all I want, a when, not a lecture on sleuthing or listening skills, just a when?"

"Over breakfast," McMoose answered.

"I didn't get any breakfast."

There are times when I really should listen. I was sure Lord McBedbugs had said the hotel was a rental over breakfast, but I can't possibly follow every tiny detail when hunger is attacking me.

However, with a mind like mine, there is always an easy solution, even to the most absurd and far-fetched story I had ever heard. I had the solution.

I smiled at Countess Von Nibbles.

"Well now," I said to her, "Now, that we know what is going on and what Lord McBedbugs is up to, can't you just evict Lord McBedbugs from the hotel?"

"What good does that do?" she asked me.

"True, he knows where the treasure is," McMoose said, "he won't stop until he gets it, but..."

McMoose looked pleased. He actually smiled at me. I think he was even...proud of me. He placed a paw on his tie, straightened it and smiled at Countess Von Nibbles and Captain Green Beard.

"You know," he began, "I am...shocked to say this...but... I think McCuddles is actually on to..."

He never finished his sentence. I have no idea what I was actually on to, but I know, it was probably clever.

The whole hotel shook from the sound of a loud explosion

Suddenly I saw a confused look on McMoose's face. I watched as he disappeared through a large hole that had formed below his feet.

He was gone.

I felt my empty belly shudder and my fur stand on end.

He had our train tickets home in his pocket. I was sure of that. In addition, he knew the way home. The worst part about his disappearance down into the hole was the fact he hadn't finished his sentence, about me being on to something.

Sometimes he can be so selfish.

Chapter 15

We all ran towards the large gap in the floor that had once held McMoose. I looked down into the smoky darkness and feared the worst.

"McMoose," I shouted into the dark hole, "you didn't finish your sentence, say something."

Only my echo replied.

"Get a light," I said to Captain Green Beard. "Hurry, I can't hear...I mean...I can't see him."

Captain Green Beard ran over to a table in the corner and grabbed a lamp. He was halfway across the room when he ran out of electrical cable. He looked at me stunned.

"Lower me down," I ordered him.

"Are ye sure laddie?" he asked me, dropping the useless lamp.

"Yes," I replied.

"It looks awfully deep," Countess Von Nibbles said, peering over the edge.

I didn't care. I wasn't about to let McMoose perish with unresolved business.

"McMoose speak to me. Finish your sentence to show us you are still alive."

Captain Green Beard lay down on his belly and crawled to the edge of the hole.

"Ye sure about this laddie?"

"Yes, lower me down, gently."

I expected him to lift me down into the hole with his long arms. He grabbed my tail and swung me across the floor and into the hole.

"Ahhh!" I screamed dangling around the dark hole.

"How else was I supposed to lower you?" he shouted above me.

I hit my head off a concrete wall and screamed up in pain, "Be careful there's not enough room down here to swing a cat."

"Aye laddie, ye be a brave sailor, even in this time of darkness, ye have time for an old joke," Captain Green Beard said.

I hit my head again and shouted up to him, "It's not an old joke, I'm serious, hold me steady."

"I found a candle," Countess Von Nibbles announced.

I heard a match light and some movement above me. Captain Green Beard's free hand lowered the lit candle into the darkness.

"What can you see?" Countess Von Nibbles asked him.

"A cat's bum," Captain Green Beard replied.

"Give me the candle," I said, reaching back with my paw.

I grabbed the candle from his hand and lowered it as far as my paw would allow. I saw bits of concrete blocks and a something small and blue below me.

"Is that you McMoose?" I shouted down.

I heard a cough.

"McMoose are you there?"

"Where else would I be?" he shouted up to me.

"You're alive, McMoose, it's a miracle."

"No miracle," he said, "I'm pinned under some rubble. Now get me out of here."

My eyes focused on the dim light from the candle. I saw McMoose more clearly. He wasn't that far down from me. But a large brick was covering his right leg and he was surrounded by...

"HOT DOGS," I gasped.

Lord McBedbugs had yummy hot dogs and all he offered us was toast for breakfast.

"Have you gone mad?" McMoose shouted up at me. "That's...dyna-"

"Drop me," I shouted at Captain Green Beard.

I hoped he had mustard stashed down here.

He let go of my tail and I crashed downwards into a bed of hot dogs. The candle fell from my paw and went out. It didn't matter.

Once the smoke and dust settled my nose would find them and then a pot of warm water to cook them in. Yummy, I was starving. I was sure I smelled mustard.

"You can't eat," Countess Von Nibbles shouted down at me.

Her words echoed in my ears.

She had to ruin it. I knew there were at least twenty yummy sticks surrounding me before the lights went out.

Suddenly, a light came on in the cellar and a voice said from behind me, "You're too late,"

I looked over my shoulder and saw the rest of the cellar. It was crammed full of boxes of food and tubes of pancake mixture. Standing between all of this was Lord McBedbugs.

"One more explosion and I will be standing above all the treasure," he said.

In his left hand, he had a hot dog with a piece of string coming out of the top of it. He flicked his right hand and I saw a small flame appear from a match.

"It will take you hours to cook that hot dog with a match," I said, from experience.

"As I tried to tell you," McMoose said, before coughing, "that's...dynamite...all around us."

I turned and looked at McMoose, "The spicy flavored dynamite kind of hot dogs?"

"Yes, McCuddles," Lord McBedbugs said, "the type that will blow your taste buds away."

"You know what you have to do?" McMoose called out.

"Eat all of them?" I said to McMoose. "But I can't...I mean...I want to eat them all...and I could...but I can't...I will turn into a vampire."

Lord McBedbugs started laughing and then lit the string on the spicy hot dog. "So long cat and mouse, it's been...umm...to coin a phrase...it has been a blast."

"Not very original," McMoose scoffed.

"What do I care, once I throw this stick of dynamite with the other sticks of dynamite and shelter from the blast, you and your stupid cat will be dessert for the flies and I will be rich."

"So they aren't really hot dogs?" I asked Lord McBedbugs.

He just laughed at me.

"Stop him McCuddles," McMoose shouted. "If you don't stop him, both you and I and the city below us will be doomed."

Lord McBedbugs stepped back and readied his arm to throw the...thing in his hand at us. He was too far away for me to pounce and attack him.

"Stop him now," McMoose cried. "Do something, anything...you have to save us and the city below us...do anything...even..."

I knew what he was saying. I had no choice. Many lives depended on me. Even if I wasn't a hundred percent convinced it wasn't a yummy hot dog about to be thrown at us.

I waved my right paw in the air and shouted out the first magic spell my hungry brain could manage and aimed it at Lord McBedbugs.

"Meow, meow dessert island for you, meow, meow."

I think, I said the wrong spell.

A sea of custard appeared on the floor beside McBedbugs. Followed by a beach of apple tart and growing upwards from the apple tart was a rocky road. The rocky road led to a marshmallow mountain with ice cream at the peak. Some multi-colored chocolate sprinkles started to rain down over the ice cream.

"Desert!" McMoose screamed at me. "Desert Island. Not a DESSERT ISLAND!"

The dessert looked nice.

The chocolate sprinkles turned from rain into a snow flurry, of multi-colored sweets. A mini tornado of maple syrup was swirling around the ice cream at the peak of the marshmallow mountain.

"Imbeciles," Lord McBedbugs shouted. "You will perish in this sugary mess and I will have the treasure."

Lord McBedbugs was about to release the stick from his hand.

"McCuddles now, before he drops the dynamite," screamed McMoose.

Charlie McMoose was more concerned about getting rid of Lord McBedbugs than my having a swim in the sea of custard. It wasn't fair. I wanted to swim in the custard sea and climb the mountain, one bite at a time.

I never get to have any fun. It is okay for me to swim in the dirty water when McMoose needs his boat rowed but not when I want to see how soft and tasty custard is to swim in.

"Goodbye you ugly cat," Lord McBedbugs said laughing.

"I am not ugly," I shouted. I waved my right paw and screamed "Meow, meow DESERT Island for you, meow, meow."

He vanished before he released the stick. That's what he gets for saying I am ugly. I am the cutest cat in the world, there isn't a mirror that doesn't love me and send me Valentine's Day cards.

McMoose let out a sigh of relief. "Where did you send him?"

Oops. I didn't really think the spell through.

"I am sure wherever he is, he is having a blast."

McMoose laughed. I looked at the beautiful dessert island and licked my lips.

"Help...me out of here," McMoose said.

I did. I removed the bricks around his leg and helped him to his feet.

He staggered to the stairs at the back of the cellar. I followed behind him, walking slowly past the dessert island.

The ice cream was starting to melt and very soon, an avalanche of ice cream would descend over the marshmallow mountain and cover the rocky road.

"The candle," I said at the bottom of the stairs, "Countess Von Nibbles candle, I must retrieve it for her."

"Meet me in the dining room," McMoose said and continued up the stairs.

I picked up the candle. But that wasn't my reason for stalling.

All my life, I have been told that dessert is not a meal. It's a treat.

Therefore, dessert it is not an actual food, but sugar and stuff, and that is not food, because it is bad for you, and dinner is never bad for you, so dessert can't be food. Right?

Of course, I am right. It makes sense then to assume that dessert is not an actual food. Therefore, if I eat some, I won't turn into a vampire.

So, I took a pawful of ice cream and stuffed it into my mouth. Followed by some marshmallows, some rocky rock and I washed it all down with some custard. I skipped the apple tart because technically that has apples in it and they are a fruit, and that makes them a food. I'm not that foolish.

A coating of sugar had attached itself to my teeth. I felt a little bit jittery and hyperactive from all the sugar. I knew it was a sign to stop. I kept eating. I deserved my dessert. I had just saved an entire city of hamsters from having their roof caving in on them and losing their lights.

"Are you coming back up, laddie?" Captain Green Beard shouted down to me.

I took one last pawful and waved goodbye to the Dessert Island.

I will miss my stay there.

"Burp...I mean yes."

My belly hurt it was that full. I struggled to the stairs.

My heart was beating too fast. Something was wrong with me.

I felt...different.

Chapter 16

With my belly nicely stuffed, I found a dusty McMoose in the dining room, giving orders on the phone to Ann. He hung up the phone and smiled proudly at Countess Von Nibbles.

"The explosion didn't harm the roof of the city," he said smiling, "Ann and the submarine crew are on their way here to safely remove the dynamite."

"And what of Lord McBedbugs?" she asked him.

He looked at me and grinned. "McCuddles sent him off somewhere and I think we won't have to worry about him, anymore."

A thank you would have been nice. I didn't care. I wasn't feeling right. I was getting sleepy from all the sugar. I really needed a nap.

"I think it is time I stopped my silly ways and honor my family," Captain Green Beard said.

"I don't understand," McMoose said.

"My great...grandfather protected the vampire hamster city. Each generation of my family did the same until I came along. I wanted to be a pirate like him. But, I have no belly for breaking the law and to be honest I suffer from sea-sickness. My family has been disgraced by my neglect of your city." He looked directly at Countess Von Nibbles and asked, "If you don't mind, I wish to stay here and rent the hotel from you and fix the submarine I accidently sunk?"

"What about your ship and your shipmates?" she asked him.

"They will be happy to have a steady job and my ship will make a great attraction bringing visitors to this wonderful place."

"Then it's settled," she beamed, "it will be so nice to have families with their children running around this big hotel."

"So laddie," he turned and looked at me, "do ye want a job?"

"Like get up really early in the morning and cook breakfast kind of a job?" I asked him.

"Aye laddie, if ye so desire, or scrubbing the decks for all the little sailors and their parents."

I didn't want to be rude to him.

"Can I think about it?" I asked instead.

As if, I wanted to live in damp and cold, eating weevils for breakfast. Not for me. A sailor's life is not for me, even if the ship is stuck on the beach.

The mere thoughts of the beach made me think of the sea of custard. My belly flip-flopped and my teeth started to hurt, not that they weren't already hurting. Now I know why some people skip dessert.

"Aye laddie, think it over. After all your help, the door to me ship is always open for you and there will always be a good meal for a good cat like yourself."

"Thank you," I said and quickly changed the subject. "So McMoose, is the case solved?"

"Indeed," he replied. "Indeed."

"So that's a yes?"

"Indeed."

"Then we can pack and go home?"

"Indeed."

Finally, I was going home. I know the beds in the hotel were massive, but I wanted away from here and away from any more offers of work.

I went to our room and got our bags while McMoose made some telephone calls. I think he wanted to look important.

I packed and struggled down the stairs with all the bags to say goodbye to Captain Green Beard and Countess Von Nibbles and all her family.

Ann gave me a big hug. I felt sad saying goodbye to Ann, she was annoying, but I liked her.

Frank was quiet.

"Don't worry," I said to him, "I won't eat any food and become a vampire. I have a strong will and never give in to temptation."

Count Von Nibbles apologized for all his lies about pretending to be a ghost.

I told him I understood that he was protecting his family and their city.

"I always," I said to him, "seek other solutions and never lie."
He smiled.

"You will visit us again?" Ann asked me.

I gave her a long hard stare and smiled.

"Of course," I lied.

We left them cheering and laughing and headed outside and set off for home. I took the three bags of garlic Countess Von Nibbles had brought for me and carried them and McMoose's bags to the bus station. I was still in his employ until we got home so what choice did I have.

He never said a word to me as we walked to the bus station.

There was no mention of a thank you or a well-done McCuddles. That's what I get for saving everyone, silence, and a sickly belly. I think the custard was souring my belly.

He just trotted ahead of me waving his umbrella around as he admired the flowers on the side of the road. Although he should have paid more attention to the direction, he was leading us in. I was sure we passed the same patch of flowers, twice.

Of course, when we climbed onto the bus, McMoose took the seat by the window and denied me my reflection on the journey home.

He snored loudly all the way home. I was wide-awake and thinking about the huge amount of pancakes, I was going to eat when it was safe to do so. Although I might go lightly on the maple syrup, my belly was still a bit off, from all the sugar.

I think all the sugar in my system had me alert and twitchy. My fangs felt larger, it must have been the sugar coating on them that made them fell bigger.

When we made it to the door of our apartment, I got excited. I was home.

My mirror was waiting for me to honor me with my reflection. How it can survive without seeing me is a mystery even McMoose can't solve.

I knew Susie was going to give me a big hug. I bet she missed me more than I missed my own reflection.

However, I had one question for McMoose that needed to be addressed now that we had made it to our...address and before we stepped inside our...home.

"Before we go in," I said to him, "the magic...I used it without permission...that's against the law, you know...without permission from a witch...and what with Susie having no license."

"I will inform the proper persons presently. I believe you may get a small fine given the circumstances...there is no excuse for breaking the law."

"But...I saved everyone. If I hadn't the city would have been-"

"Doesn't make it right."

"It isn't fair, they will take my fur...the cold...ugly...no Charlie...it isn't fair."

"I will suggest to them you only get community service this time and not insist on fur removal, but only because I don't want to listen to you whine on and on for weeks."

"What's community service? Is that like...doing work?"

"Who knows McCuddles. You might get lucky and only do litter duty," he said opening the door. "You helped me save a city, so I will do all I can to make sure you won't lose...all your fur, again."

Loss of fur was the terrible price for using magic without permission. It does grow back, but it itches and denies me any mirror time.

I can't look at myself bald. I can't face that, not again.

Well if McMoose wanted to be mean, so could I.

"You're just sore because Lord McBedbugs hired you and because he was the baddie you didn't get paid."

"I just said, I would help you."

So he did.

"What I meant is, Charlie will you get paid?"

He turned and looked at me.

"Actually, you are wrong; well you are right...but wrong."

"Huh?"

"About getting paid."

"What?"

I hate getting confused. I blamed the sugar.

"You forget...Lady McBedbugs," he said.

"How can I forget someone we never saw?"

"Well while you were retrieving my bags I phoned her, and she said she was happy to pay me for getting rid of her husband. It seems she didn't like him very much. She does want to know where he ended up so she can get the divorce papers signed."

"Then she should pay me. It was my spell that sent him away."

"Indeed, but you work for me not the other way around," he said, entering the kitchen.

"So how much did she pay you to send her husband off to a deserted island?"

"I get nothing," he said to the floor. "I did this job for one reason only...for Susie."

He looked at me and smiled.

"She is the most generous person in the world...I made a deal with the Witch's Council on her behalf to buy back her license."

I was stunned and speechlessness.

"Now, I am terribly tired and must make some phone calls, goodnight McCuddles."

He took his bags from my paws, left me alone in the kitchen, and went to his bedroom. One part of me wanted to hate how cruel he had been to me.

But how could I hate him?

He was going to make Susie a witch again.

I dropped my bags of garlic on the floor and crawled over to my mirror under the blanket in my basket. I had to do something while I waited for Susie to come home from work.

I rubbed the mirror with my paw and said hello to it.

My mirror didn't reply.

"Hello, hello," I said waving at the mirror. "Did you miss me?"

Nothing.

Maybe the mirror was upset because I had been away from it for a long time. It must be terrible not to see my cuteness, every day.

I gave the mirror my full attention. All I saw reflected in the mirror was the back of the kitchen. I waved my paw in front of the mirror, again.

Still nothing. I wasn't there.

I mean I was there. It was I in front of the mirror, but the mirror wasn't reflecting me.

I got a horrible feeling in my belly. Worse than hunger.

"My reflection is gone," I screamed.

I heard a noise behind me. I hoped it was my reflection playing peek-a-boo.

"I'm home," Susie said, opening the front door.

I dropped the mirror and ran over to her. I jumped up into her arms.

I tried to speak, but the shock was too much for me. The words didn't want to come out.

"My...my..." was all I could say.

"McCuddles," she cried, hugging me tightly. "I didn't expect such a welcome home from you. You really missed me."

"My...my..."

"I know, I know, I missed you too."

"My...my..."

"Witch, I know I am your witch again. Isn't it wonderful? Charlie phoned me earlier, isn't it good news. I will be a witch again. We can do good and help children find their missing teddies bears."

"I..."

"Speechless, so unusual for you, the good news must be too much for you. I can't wait to go good-witching again."

I shook my head. "My...re..."

"I know Jack...you think that the reason...the reason for your existence is to do evil...but you know I don't like to do evil spells, Jack. We make a good team doing good. We can do a lot of good together Jack. Oh, Jack, I am so happy."

She hugged the air out of me.

"My..."

"Your witch Jack, I know...it's wonderful. Now, where is Charlie? I must thank him."

"Here I am," McMoose shouted.

"Oh Charlie," she greeted him, by dropping me like a bag of potatoes onto the floor.

"My...me...listen to me," I shouted up at her.

"I hope he wasn't bold," she said, looking at me and then at McMoose.

"No...He did help...a little," McMoose replied.

"A little, I saved the day and...now my...my..."

"I know Jack, your belly is empty and you are hungry, I will make you some pancakes," Susie said.

"He can't eat...he was bitten by a vampire...he is not allowed food for a week," McMoose said.

"Actually," I said correcting him, "it is only six days...not that it matters...but...my reflection...it's terrible."

"Not really," McMoose said, "we look at your ugly mug every day and get by. I am sure you will eventually adapt to your ugly-"

"I am not ugly. It's gone," I cried.

"What is Jack?" Susie asked.

"My reflection..."

My whole body shuddered. Tears fell from my eyes.

McMoose smiled. "How do you know you aren't ugly if you have no reflection?"

I hate him.

"I want my reflection back," I shouted.

"Did you eat anything?" McMoose asked me.

"Umm...no," I replied to him and then looked at Susie, with my feed me, hug me and do what I want now cutest face. "Susie, you can magic me better?"

"He's telling fibs," McMoose said, placing his paws on his waist. "You ate some of the dessert. They don't call me Charles McMoose the sleuth for nothing."

"Dessert is not a food," I cried at him.

"It kind of is," Susie said.

"You don't call it food when I ask for some. You call it a treat that has no goodness in it."

"True," Susie smiled. "Dessert isn't really a food group. However, it is made with things like eggs and flour, and they are foods. Foods drowned in excessive amounts of sugar. Too much sugar, to be healthy. But, they are a food. Oh, silly Jack, what have you done?"

"Stop," I cried. "You are confusing me, it doesn't matter what a food is or isn't. I need my reflection back."

McMoose walked over to the three bags of garlic on the floor. He took out one huge clove of garlic out of the bag.

He stood smiling at me with the clove of garlic in his hand.

"Nibble on this," he said. "And then you will have to starve yourself for a week to get your reflection back."

"Six days," I corrected him.

I took the garlic from his paw. It smelled horrible.

I took a huge chunk, chewed and swallowed followed by another and another till all the bags were empty. I felt it work straight away. I ran to my basket and lifted my mirror.

Slowly the cutest cat in the world greeted me from the mirror. I smiled at him and he smiled back.

The mirror loves me. I felt warm all over. I am so cute. Really, I am.

My fur is so shiny and soft. I looked at Susie. I needed a cuddle.

However, before I was able to lift my front two paws up in the universal sign for cuddle-me-now, something black fell over my eyes.

A clump of hair from my head fell to the floor. Followed by another. I turned to the mirror and saw the light shine off the top of my head.

"I'm bald!" I screamed.

McMoose looked away from me.

"You phoned them," I screamed at him. "You told on me, didn't you?"

"Yes, I did. I must report any crime at the first available opportunity, but don't panic, they said that because you helped save so many vampire hamsters, that your punishment would only be half baldness for a month."

I shivered.

"Susie, help me?"

She didn't.

"Sorry Jack, the law is the law," was all she said.

"A hat," McMoose announced.

"What?" I shouted at him.

"You can wear a hat. I have a wooly green hat you can use with a bobble on it."

"Oh Charlie," Susie said. "You really are a kind mouse to share with Jack."

"I'm starving," McMoose said.

"Me too," Susie agreed. "What shall we eat?"

"Well I am not a big fan of pancakes," McMoose said, looking at me. "But, I actually wouldn't mind some right about now."

Susie made the nicest smelling and the biggest pancakes I ever saw in my life. She even opened a fresh bottle of real maple syrup.

I watched McMoose drown his pancakes with the maple syrup. Then with his knife, he sliced each pancake, slowly. He had five of them, and even more slowly, he stuffed each piece into his greedy wee mouth.

He did all this while my belly rumbled.

He even licked his plate clean.

I was happy to see him leave the table and go to bed. I hoped he would get a bellyache. But I never get what I want.

Instead, he returned to the kitchen with the wooly hat in his paws.

"This will keep your head warm," he said, placing the wooly hat on my head.

"Say thank you to Charlie," Susie said.

I wanted to claw his furry head off his shoulders.

"Thank you, Charlie," I muttered instead.

"Goodnight...McBaldy," McMoose whispered, before scampering off to his room laughing.

"Goodnight Jack," Susie said to me. "Get some sleep. We have lots of work to do tomorrow now that I am a witch again."

I watched her leave. I felt alone and hungry.

I crawled over to my basket and turned the mirror away from me. I was too hideous to look at. The hat looked stupid and every time I moved, the bobble...bobbled and hit me in the nose.

I got into my basket and pulled the blankets over my whole body. I closed my eyes.

The hat kept itching. I took the hat off a few times, but then my head became frozen from the lack of fur covering.

I felt like I was getting brain freeze, without the nice ice cream taste that usually goes with brain freeze. I was hungry and cold.

I hate my life.

I had saved the world, yet again, and here I was, wearing a hideous green wooly hat with a bobble. This is no way for the cutest, magical cat in the world to live.

I want to live in a castle surrounded by maple trees (to get maple syrup from) with an endless supply of pancakes on my table. I should have servants catering to my every whim.

I want to nap when I want, eat when I want and do evil when I want.

Someday, my dreams will come true.

Until then, a cat can dream.

Well, that is if I ever get to sleep with a cold itchy head and an empty belly.

Jack will return.

(Before you go, Lord McBedbugs is alive. He was able to extinguish the stick of dynamite in his hand. He suffered some burns to his fingertips and is currently in hiding from his wife and the police.)

35080731R00061

Made in the USA
Middletown, DE
18 September 2016